JUST
GO

A NOVEL BY
GUY A. CARROZZO

"JUST GO"
Copyright © 2019
by
Guy A. Carrozzo

MYSELF PUBLISHING

Other book by Guy Carrozzo:

"Left Coast Coach"

"Hunting Hollwood"

Available on Amazon.com

COVER ART: By Guy A. Carrozzo

Dedicated to
Vince and Doug,
who both died too young.

PREFACE

This story is loosely based on my time at Humboldt State University during the 1975-76 school year. It was a great experience both academically and socially. It was the first time that I lived away from home. To be in an area with such rich natural beauty only added to the experience.

The names of the characters and most of the dialogue are fictitious. At a few points in the story, the characters will turn to the reader to give a further explanation of their thoughts or actions. The sentences that are in *italics* are the character's thoughts at that moment.

Also in the story, references are made to certain singers and their music. The lyrics of those songs can help set the mood of the scene. If the reader is unfamiliar with the songs mentioned, they might listen to those songs or at least look up the lyrics online.

Like the characters in the story, most people try to plan their futures, but events outside their control end up guiding their path into the unknown.

CHAPTER 1
Go Where?

September 1973

"Go."

"Okay, but what is it like?"

"Just go."

"But is it hard to get the classes you need to graduate? You know, like they say it is at Southwestern State?"

"Have you ever been to Sequoia State?"

"No."

"Then I can't explain it to you. You just need to experience it for yourself to understand."

"Well, I need to select the right college...you know, for my future."

"There's nowhere you can be that isn't where you're meant to be. John Lennon said that."

"I don't think it is wise to have one of the Beatles select my college."

"You are so pathetic. It's about experiencing life. Trying new things. Seeing new places. Expanding your mind. Going to class is only a small part of the college experience."

"Hey, if you think I am going to try hallucinogens, you're crazy. I am not going to take drugs and mess up my future."

"That's right. Listen to mommy and daddy. Are you a first-born child?"

"Yes, but why is that important? Don't you see, I am trying to find my destiny."

"You don't 'find' your destiny. Your destiny finds you. Your character reveals the destiny you're supposed to have. Heraclitus said that, or something close to it.   Think of it this way...you've been on a train since you started school. The train has stayed on the tracks the whole time going from grade to grade until you graduate from high school. Then the train jumps the tracks and you can go wherever you want to go to college."

"Usually, when the train jumps the tracks, they call it a train wreck. I'm not even sure where it's at."

"Hey dip-shit.   Never end a sentence with a preposition. You'll never get into college if you don't know basic grammar."

"But I hear it rains a lot up there."

"Have you ever walked through a redwood forest, with ferns all dripping with a steady drizzle of rain? Smelled the air when the pine needles are wet? Felt the breeze as you look up to the canopy of treetops and it blows the rain drops onto your face?"

"No."

"Rain is a small price to pay for such beauty. I went there for one year and it was the best year of my life. It is a whole different world. I wish I could have stayed there longer than I did. Things just didn't work out for me. I had to come back home. But I'd go back in a minute if I had the chance. If you're looking for your 'destiny,' then go. If you just want to take classes, then stay."

SPEAKING TO THE READER...

What you have to understand is that I have known this kid for a long time. Don't get me wrong; he's a good guy. But he is very naïve. He isn't hanging on to his mother's coat strings; he's hanging on to the umbilical cord. He really needs to get away from here, go out on his own, and grow up. Kids just a few years older than him were drafted and went to Vietnam. They killed other people and saw their own comrades and friends killed at the hands of the enemy. This kid probably has his mom select the clothes he wears to school each day.

Going away to school would be a great experience for him. It would be a version of boot camp that he could survive. Having to plan his week, budget his money, and do his own laundry would go a long way in teaching him to be independent. At least the cafeteria will take the place of "mommy" so he won't starve to death.

There are several things I worry about though. First, he is a bit of a smart ass. He isn't disrespectful, but he is bright and points out contradictions all around him. I think he does it because he craves attention. He isn't loud, but he comments on things he sees before he thinks about the consequences. He is also a bit of a prankster. Not a malicious prankster, but enough of one to get him in trouble. Also, if he gets involved with someone—he is a bit naïve as I have mentioned before. Not that he will find someone in the first place. There aren't any Southern California Barbie Doll-types at Sequoia State. And the people up there are different too. They are earthier, maybe spiritual—but not necessarily religious. I don't know how this kid, who grew up in the shadow of the Matterhorn at Disneyland, will react to all that. He's going to be disappointed when he gets up there and finds out that real animals don't dance and real flowers don't sing. It will be a real culture shock to him.

"I will say this about him; he is honest and tries to do the right thing. But sometimes that blows up in his face. I say he's got a fifty-fifty chance of surviving up there—but if he does, he will be better for it."

———————

Anthony and his classmates were born in the mid-fifties at the height of post-war optimism. Jobs were plentiful—for white males, whether they had high school diplomas or college degrees. This was partially true because over 400,000 U.S. servicemen had been killed in World War II and partially because Europe was still recovering from the destruction of the war. The U.S. was one of the few countries that were making everything from refrigerators to truck tires for themselves and the rest of the world. The U.S. was producing all the new products one's mind could conceive of for families in the nuclear age.

Then the sixties came along and it was a decade of change. His generation watched people, who hadn't been sharing in the post-war euphoria, wanting their share of the American Dream. Black people, brown people, Native American people, women, gays, all wanted what white Americans had been enjoying for the previous two decades. Against this cultural upheaval, both the best and worst aspect of America were revealed in two long-running events—the race to land a man on the moon and the Vietnam War. The soundtrack for this young generation was for the first time generated from the consumer up, instead of from the record company executives down. Groups like The Beatles; The Rolling Stones; Crosby, Stills and Nash; and Country Joe and the Fish all expressed what the young people of the country were feeling in their souls.

The revolution of the sixties spilled over into the seventies. Yet even as Anthony became a teenager, he still hadn't emerged from his socially insulated, perfect, Disney-like environment, and had no idea what was happening in the real world.

March 30, 1974

Dear Anthony:

Congratulations. It is with great pleasure
that I offer you admission to Sequoia State
University for the fall term of the 1974 school
year.

Your impressive application and many
accomplishments convinced us that you would be
a success at Sequoia State. We realize that
you might be accepted at several institutions
of higher learning, and we hope that you take
time to learn more about the SSU campus and
community. In that regard, we invite you to
attend our open house for prospective students
on May 6th and 7th.

Please remember your acceptance is contingent
on your continued academic achievement and
final official transcripts from your high
school registrar. Once your final transcripts
are received, you will receive a planning guide
for your freshman year class schedule. We also
urge incoming freshmen to consider on-campus
housing. Please contact our Housing Office for
more information. Again, congratulations and
welcome to Sequoia State University.

Sincerely,

Susan DuBoise

Susan DuBoise, Admissions Counselor
Sequoia State University

"Mom? MOM! Did I apply to Sequoia State?"

"I think so dear. You applied to so many places, it is hard to remember."

"Where is Sequoia State again?"

"Northern California, I think. Or maybe by Santa Cruz?"

"But all my friends are going to Southwestern State in San Diego."

"Well, as your mom, you know I would love for you to go to Southwestern since it is so close to home. I'm thrilled that they accepted you."

———

April 1974

"Okay, that's all for today, but remember, we have a test on Chapter 23 on Friday. And no one leaves class until the bell rings."

"Ah, come on Mr. Penner! Let us go early just once."

"Yeah, come on, just this once. They're giving out our graduation announcements in the quad and there is gonna be a million people!"

"How many of you are seniors?"

"Just six of us. Come on, let us go."

"Okay, wait—I'll let you go two minutes early, but if any campus supervisor or assistant principal stops you, you have to say you're from Mrs. Smithson's class, not from mine."

"It's a deal, Mr. Penner. You're so cool."

"Okay, the next person who calls me cool, I am NOT letting you go early."

"You are so NOT cool Mr. Penner."

"So Anthony, where are you going to college next year. I heard you were accepted at several places," Mr. Penner questioned.

"I'm still not sure. Southwestern is where I will probably go—close to home and all."

"Where else are you considering?"

"Sequoia State."

"That's in Northern California, isn't it? Go there."

"Why? Have you been there Mr. Penner?"

"No. But I can tell you this. Southwestern State is a good school, but basically you will have the same experience you've had for the past four years over again for the next four or five years. Southwestern for you will be like high school with ashtrays. You'll be in the same environment, same friends, and still living at home—a very safe decision, but not a brave one. Remember the end of 'American Graffiti?' Who do you want to be, Steve or Curt?"

Penner turned to the rest of the class, "Okay seniors, you can go early. Remember, if you're caught, you're from Mrs. Smithson's class, not mine." The students loved that little bit of larceny from the mostly stoic Mr. Penner.

CHAPTER 2
Think I'm Gonna Miss You

<u>June 1974</u>

It was going to be a busy month for the seniors. The prom, baccalaureate, and graduation all were occurring in the next three weeks. Graduation announcements were ordered long ago, been addressed, and were in the mail. Cap and gowns had all been ordered and delivered. Prom dresses had been purchased and tuxes had been rented.

Anthony only had two serious events coming up. First were final exams—which determined final grades and in turn affected one's transcripts, of which final copies were sent to the colleges where students had been accepted—and that acceptance was contingent on those final grades.

And second, telling Judy he was going away to college. At least he was pretty sure. He had actually been accepted at both Sequoia State and Southwestern State. He had only applied for housing at Sequoia because if he decided to go to Southwestern, he would be living at home and commuting.

Anthony and Judy were going to double date to the prom with Tim, Anthony's best friend and his girlfriend, Ginny. Anthony had been dating Judy since the beginning of the school year. It was nice to come out of the locker room after a football game on a chilly night and have a warm body to hug you, win or lose. Tim had been dating Ginny since their sophomore year when they were both in the marching band. Ginny was still in the band, but Tim was no longer a band member as he wanted to concentrate on football.

It was decided that they would use Tim's car for the prom. It was a dark blue, 1965 Ford Falcon four-door sedan. After school on the Thursday before the prom, they met at Tim's house to wash the car. They detailed it pretty good, washing the exterior, which cleaned it but didn't do much for the paint that was flaking off it in many places. While Tim washed the car, Anthony took a bucket and brush and cleaned the tires as best he could. Together they cleaned the windows. Then they pulled the car in the garage and put on a coat of car wax, which again didn't do much for the poor paint job but did make it look shinier. Then, borrowing Tim's mom's canister vacuum, they cleaned the interior of the car, getting out the sand and grit that had accumulated in the corners of the floor. Anthony put just a little car wax on the back seat, which was made of vinyl and buffed it out. It made the seat shiny and slick. They got permission from Tim's dad to park the car in the garage on Thursday and Friday nights before the prom on Saturday.

Friday after school, the pair went down to Keith's Tux shop in downtown and picked up their tuxes. At the store, they both tried them on to make sure everything fit. Tim's tux was more traditional and when he came out of the dressing room, he looked kind of like James Bond.

Anthony had opted for a tux that came with black pants and a coat that was a black, white and blue plaid. It was loud and looked like he was a trombone player in a big band group. Both boys thought they looked great.

The flower shop was first on the list for Saturday morning. The corsages were each boxed in gold boxes and kept in Tim's mom's refrigerator. The boys each went home to have lunch and take a nap in the early afternoon. At 3 p.m., Anthony's mom woke him up so he could get ready. Anthony jumped in the shower and while the hot water was spraying over him, he tried to think of how he would break the news to Judy. He hoped it would not break her heart. He certainly didn't want to ruin the night for her or Tim and Ginny.

After the shower, he dried off and started getting dressed. He put on the black pants. They had a darker stripe down the side. Then came the ruffled shirt and the button studs and cufflinks. Next were the cummerbund, black socks and patent leather shoes. Finally, he put on the black, white and blue plaid jacket. He looked in the mirror. *I look like Doc Severinsen*, he thought. *Bitchen*.

Downstairs his mom gushed and sister Anne teased. Dad took half a roll of film on his Instamatic camera.

"Now remember, we want Tim's parents to make double copies of all the group shots they take of you all. We'll pay them back of course," Mom said adding the financial provision.

There was a knock at the door and when his sister opened it, James Bond stood there looking so dapper. She shrieked with glee.

"Come in Tim," Mom yelled from the kitchen. Tim came striding into the kitchen and stood next to Anthony. Dad took more photos until he ran out of flashcubes. "Now you boys have a good time and don't forget your corsages. You'd break those girls hearts if you did."

Anthony jumped in the Falcon and Tim drove back to his house. The girls' parents were dropping them off so they too could get some photos.

Judy wore a long, pink chiffon dress. Ginny wore a halter-top gown which was a departure from the more conservative knee-length dresses with buttons and collars that girls wore to school.

Instead of regular, everyday lip-gloss and mascara, both girls wore eyeliner, green eye shadow and frosted pink lipstick, which made them appear more mature than their years. They had been transformed from girls to women in the three hours it took them to get ready.

The corsages were taken out of cold storage and dutifully pinned on the girls. There must have been a dozen people on the front lawn taking photos from every angle. The boys stood next to their dates while no less than five cameras captured their every move. The prom goers were running out of patience at just the same time as the parents ran out of film, so it worked out perfectly. The kids dashed into the car while the parents and siblings milled about a bit and the mothers wiped their eyes with tissue.

Anthony opened the door for both Judy and Ginny, then tucked in their dresses before closing the car doors and departing for the dance.

The prom itself didn't start until 8 p.m. but there was still the tradition of going out to dinner. They went to Kim's Café, which was near the beach and served a variety of American and Italian dishes. Tim had made reservations early in the week and since it was only a little after 5 p.m. they were ushered to a table for four right away.

The waiters served them attentively and as expected, at the end of the meal, the young diners only left a minimum tip. As the busboys cleared their table, there was still most of the food left behind.

Back in the car, Anthony thought the time was right to break the big news.

"Ah, Judy—I think I told you that I got accepted at several colleges."

"Uh huh. Why are these seats so slippery?" she asked sliding her rump back and forth on the waxed seat. The chiffon material added to the slipperiness.

"Yes, I waxed them, but I also told you that one of the schools was Sequoia State up north."

"Hey Ginny, watch me slide back and forth on the seat Anthony waxed," Judy called out.

"So I am thinking about going away to school next year. I am thinking of going to Sequoia State," Anthony repeated.

"Are your seats as slippery?" Judy asked Ginny.

"Did you hear what I said, Judy? I might go away to school."

"Yes, I heard you. That's pretty cool," Judy said calmly. She was not sure why Anthony was being so dramatic.

"Well, I just wanted you to know. I hope it won't dampen your spirits tonight."

"Nah. Let's go have fun," and she playfully leaned over and kissed Anthony on the cheek. Then she screamed with delight as she slid away from Anthony on the slick seat as Tim turned a sharp left into the parking a lot of the hotel that was hosting the prom.

With prom tickets in hand, the two couples walked into the lobby of the luxurious ballroom suite and stood in line as a single student council member, seated at a folding table, used a ruler to cross out the names of the prom-goers as they presented their tickets.

While Judy and Ginny chatted, Anthony confided in Tim and told him, "I think Judy is taking the news pretty hard. I hope I haven't hurt her feelings."

The dance featured a live band who played many current hits as well as favorite oldies. Most of the songs were fast and the students shimmied, shook and wiggled to the beat. When the band played their version of the Beach Boys song, "Surfin' USA" everyone went wild! Later, the Beatles song, "Hey Jude" allowed everyone to slow dance. Anthony held Judy close on the dance floor as they gently rocked back and forth to the music. He hoped that his going away to school wouldn't ruin his relationship with her.

CHAPTER 3
Big Mistake?

September 1974

He set his trunk and suitcases down in the hallway in front of his assigned dorm room and took the key out of the envelope with his name scrawled on it. He tried to fit the key in the lock in the center of the doorknob, but it stuck. He flipped the key over and tried again. The door opened and he left the key in the lock and carried the two suitcases into the room and let them drop from his hands, still upright, onto the floor on each side of him. He sat down on the dark brown suitcase and looked around the empty dorm room. There was an open window opposite the door. Two beds with bare, lumpy mattresses, two empty dressers, two metal desks—one with a large chip in the corner of the linoleum desktop. The bare cinderblock walls painted white. A few empty clothes hangers swayed rhythmically on the bar in the closet sounding like a soft, tinny wind chime. Home seemed so far away from this place. He looked down at the ugly blue and black shag carpet, and wondered if he had made the biggest mistake of his life.

"HEY, anyone who wants to come, we are all going to dinner at 5 down at a Mexican place in town." The announcement echoed down the dorm hallway. Many of the doors of the dorm rooms were propped open. People were carrying up two flights of stairs all of the school supplies, clothing and books they needed to face the first year of college. In both the girls' hallway and the boys' hallway, people checked their clocks or watches, put their books down, or stopped unpacking suitcases and trunks.

As most of the dorm residents were newly arrived incoming freshmen who had come from distant places around the state, the country, and a few from abroad, and none of them knew a single soul on campus, there was a stampede to meet in the first-floor lounge— the disembarking point for the trip into town. In fact, they were all 15 minutes early—as you might have expected from mostly anal-retentive, success-driven, slightly paranoid young academics. This was especially true when the speaker at the campus orientation had said to the large crowd of new students, "In college, you can study, sleep, and party. But you can only do two of those. Choose wisely. Now look at the person on your left. Now look at the person or your right. One of the three of you will not still be here by the end of the school year. Sequoia State University is a great place, but it's not for everybody."

For people who had spent their entire kindergarten through twelfth grade years striving for an excellent academic record, coming to school even when they were sick, participating in extra-curricular activities they could care less about but showed they were well-rounded, serving food to homeless people to show they were involved in community service projects—the thought of a one-third drop-out rate was, to say the least, a bit unnerving.

Most of the incoming freshmen were a bit shocked by this statistic. The first reaction was denial. "Well, it won't happen to me." But being rather intelligent, most students understood that the speaker was quoting statistics and statistics were pretty cold, hard facts. Then, the students probably reflected on what would happen next if they dropped out of college.

A college degree with a good major practically guaranteed a respectable career, a lucrative salary, and an attractive spouse—basically a great life. If they dropped out of college, the future was frightfully ambiguous.

By 5 p.m., the first-floor lounge was full of people talking amongst themselves. Jeff, one of the LGA's (while most colleges call dorm directors, Resident Advisors (R.A.s) Sequoia State called them Living Group Advisors) hollered, "Follow me," and the rule-following mob followed the LGA out of the dorm lobby, across the campus, and across the bridge that crossed over Highway 101 and down the hill into town.

As the students strolled along, they introduced themselves and conversed. They were however, unaware of their true similarities.

There were no homecoming queens or captains of the football team—they were married right out of high school.

There were no class presidents or valedictorians—they went to Ivy League schools.

There were no children of rich celebrities or corporate CEO's—they went to USC.

Here you had people, who in high school had been in FFA, drill team, drama, art, marching band and a few played sports, but there were no blue-chip athletes. They would become teachers, nurses, forest rangers, cops, or small business owners. They would become the backbone of society—not rich, not poor—working for a good but not fantastic salary, paying their taxes, and hoping for a decent retirement. Some would follow in their parents' footsteps, while others would be the first in their family to ascend into the middle class.

Some would become Democrats, and others would be Republicans, but most all would be moderates and lean towards the middle. Most hoped to do something special in their life, but did not realize that their lives were, for the most part, already predetermined or, more accurately, limited by their status in high school and their parents' status in society.

Sure, they had choices. A very few would improve their station and exceed expectations, but most would not. This age group still held on to the false belief that, "you can be whatever you want in life," and because of that, still sought their destiny and thought they could control it.

Anthony was in the middle of the pack of students as they made their way into town. As they walked, there was a multi-directional conversation going on between all members of the group. Mostly introductions, "My name is so-and-so. I'm from so-and-so." And the usual questions, "What is your major? How many classes are you taking this term?" And some of the smarter guys were asking the girls, "And how does your boyfriend feel about you going away to school? What, you don't have a boyfriend back home? I don't believe it!" This was important information to keep track of if any dorm romances were to blossom.

Anthony listened, asked questions politely, and answered questions as they were asked of him. He was observing the group as they walked past old Victorian homes and craftsmen-style bungalows, some well-kept—others with tall weeds in the yard and badly in need of care. There were about a dozen people—five girls, seven boys: two African Americans, three Hispanic, seven Caucasian. One girl in the group was slightly plump and looked like she really didn't want to be a part of all this activity. She was quiet and kept to herself for the most part. As in any group, Anthony observed there was one obvious comedian—some guy named Randall. The black girl, Keisha, was very loud, funny and seemed to enjoy bantering back and forth with Randall. Randall had apparently been around black people before and was not intimidated by Keisha. He teased her and said things that made some of the other white kids hold their breath, as they had never been exposed to black people or black culture before. When Keisha stared for a moment, and then laughed at his slightly racial or suggestive jokes; the rest of the group nervously laughed and gave a slight sigh of relief.

The Mexican restaurant, with its gaily painted exterior, was just off the town square and in between a record shop on one side and a thrift shop on the other. When Jeff told the hostess that they had a party of twelve, she said that they would have to wait a few minutes so some tables could be pushed together for a group that size. The group half stood and half sat on benches in the restaurant entry area and continued their spirited conversation.

When the hostess said the tables were ready, Anthony was detained listening to one girl nervously telling him her entire life story and how her low-life boyfriend dumped her after the first time they had sex.

Too much information, way too soon, Anthony thought to himself. He excused himself and went to the restroom as a way to politely break-off the conversation. At the sink, he washed his face and looked at himself in the mirror. He was still not sure coming to Sequoia State was a good decision.

When he returned to the group, still engaged in animated chatter, he had to grab a chair for himself from a single table and squeeze it in at the corner of the big table. Luckily, the girl who got dumped was on the opposite side and several people down from him. Jeff, the LGA, was helping the overworked waitress put baskets of tortilla chips on the heavy wooden Spanish-style table, while one of the girls in the group was helping fill water glasses for everyone. When the girl, who was wearing a tight pair of jeans and a plaid blouse, leaned in to set a glass down in front of Randall, he casually but purposely put his hand on her ass—at which point she hip-checked him away from her—which brought about a roar of laughter from the group. Randall feigned almost falling out of his chair, and the girl smiled knowingly back at him. Then she filled his water glass and set it in front of him.

Keisha chided him with a heavy fake ghetto accent, "Dat's right white-boy. And a good thing you don't try none o' dat shit with me o' you be looking for yo' teeth on da floor." Which brought another burst of laughter from everyone.

Anthony was impressed with how the girl filling the water glasses handled the situation. She made it clear that she was having none of Randall's antics; did it without saying a word; and yet did not spoil the moment that everyone was enjoying.

The dinner orders were what you might expect from college students with a limited income. A lot of a' la carte orders of enchiladas, or tacos. Randall must have been a man of means since he ordered the only full dinner—the Grande Supreme.

After dinner, the walk back to campus was a bit more subdued. The adrenaline rush of first meeting so many people had given way to more normal conversation. The large group had broken up into smaller groups that shared some commonality—either the same major; or from the same geographic area; or in a few cases, common people they knew. When they walked around the town square and started up the hill, they passed the same Victorian and craftsmen homes, which looked more foreboding in the darkness now that the sun had set.

Randall and Keisha lagged behind the group and were laughing hysterically together. No one could hear what was being said, but when people would look back at them, they were bent over in laughter. One would have thought they had too many margaritas at dinner. In reality, no one had any alcohol as no one was of drinking age, although two people did try to order bottled beer, but were carded.

Anthony was now pretty exhausted from the day's activities and just wanted to get back to his dorm room to get some sleep. In the little group up ahead, he eyed the Water Glass Girl. Someone said her name was Mary. Or was it Sue. Anyway, Anthony thought she was kind of cute.

CHAPTER 4
Getting to Know You

The next day, Anthony was up early. His door was propped open and someone's stereo was playing Loggins and Messina's hit, "Your Momma Don't Dance." There were some conversations in the hallway as people came and went. He unpacked his suitcases and trunk, and stored the luggage in the cabinet above the closet on his side of the mirror-image dorm room. The only personalizing elements he brought to decorate his room with were three posters. One was "The Langlois Bridge at Arles" by Vincent van Gogh. The other two were Picasso's—"Don Quixote" and "Bouquet with Hands." He hung some clothes in the closet, folded some other clothes and put them in the small dresser, and put his school supplies in his desk. On the wall-mounted bookshelf, he put a framed photo of Judy. He also placed a Webster's dictionary he received as a graduation gift from his grandparents on the shelf. He looked across the room and felt better about things. At least his stuff was put away and things were neat and organized. Just like a first-born would want it. Looking across to the vacant half of the room, he wondered with whom he would be sharing this abode.

As he sat back to take a break, two girls from the dinner the night before came bounding into his room. Unbeknownst to him, they had seen him tidying up his room as they walked back and forth in the hallway. When they were sure he was finished and everything was in its place, they pounced. They were both wearing well-worn overalls and loose-fitting flannel shirts—practically the school uniform at Sequoia State. Natalie, a beautiful Italian girl from Ventura, threw her softball mitt and hit Anthony right in the face. Then Natalie and her roommate, Lena, a dark-haired, olive-skinned girl, pulled every desk drawer and dresser drawer out and dumped all the clothes and school supplies in a pile in the middle of the floor. The whole time, they were laughing like banshees. They completely ransacked the place. Then, stopping suddenly, they looked at each other silently with big eyes and then they burst out laughing again. Natalie picked up her mitt and they both sprinted out of the room. Anthony could hear their hysterical laughter fade away as they ran down the hallway. *What the hell just happened*, he wondered. Using the back of his hand, he wiped a little blood from his nose where the mitt had hit him.

His roommate showed up a few days after Anthony had arrived. His name was Don. To get assigned to the dorms, every student had to fill out this long survey to match them with their roommate. It asked everything from political views, to religious views, to lifestyles. On everything that they asked, Anthony put that it didn't matter to him. He just wanted to make sure he got dorm housing—which at Sequoia State could be difficult. The only thing that he specified was he wanted a non-smoker. Well, Don comes in and tells Anthony that he played football in high school (like Anthony had), played center in fact (like Anthony had), and then proceeded to light up a cigarette. Anthony said, "Don, you can do anything you want in this room, but please don't smoke."

"You got it Bro. I've been trying to quit anyway," he replied.

A week later, classes started and students were getting into the rhythm of going to class, studying, eating, doing laundry, etc. Some were better at it than others. Some had been doing it all through high school.

Anthony had not. At home, his mom did all the cooking for him and his family. She also had done the all the laundry.

Early Saturday morning, while most people were still asleep, Anthony threw on a t-shirt and shorts, grabbed his laundry basket of dirty clothes—which by now had a ripe odor to it, a handful of quarters from the coin jar in his desk, and a travel size box of laundry soap. He then headed down to the first-floor laundry room.

Delicates. Lights. Darks. Normal. Heavy Soiled. What the hell are delicates? He thought to himself. Anthony was happy he was able to figure out which machines were washers and which were dryers. He had put his quarters in the slots on the washer and was staring at the dial. He was totally stumped as to which setting to choose. He looked at his laundry basket—a mixture of lights and darks. Nothing delicate that he could see. He thought that his smelly heap of dirty clothes probably needed hot water but there was not that choice on the dial. Deciding on "Normal" he twisted the dial. He put the entire contents of his laundry basket in the washer, dumped an unmeasured amount of laundry soap on top of the clothes, pushed the shiny slide lever that accepted the quarters, and... nothing happened. He stood there for a minute thinking that if he was smart enough to get into college, he should be able to figure out how to use a washing machine.

A voice from behind him said, "Push in the dial to make it start."

Anthony pushed the dial and the machine throbbed to life as the hose started filling the washer with hot water. Turning around, he saw a sleepy-eyed Water Glass Girl sorting her laundry into two other machines.

"Thanks," he said.

She pitched a pair of running shorts and jeans into one machine and a small lacy bra and panties in another. *Delicates,* Anthony thought.

"Sure," she said.

Anthony flipped his laundry basket over on top of the washer he was using and walked past her to the door out of the laundry room. *That went well,* he thought reassuringly to himself. He then felt guilty, so he sprinted up two flights of stairs, burst into his dorm room, sat down at his desk and started writing a letter to his girlfriend Judy back at home.

"What in the hell are you doing up so early on a Saturday morning?" Don asked as he raised his head from his pillow and opened one bleary eye.

"Nothing. Go back to sleep. Sorry."

Don's head slumped back into the pillow for a bit more shut eye.

ANTHONY SPEAKING TO THE READER...

"I know, I know. I am a horrible person. I have a girlfriend back home and I am looking at this girl that I don't even really know. I have to commit to my relationship with Judy and keep that strong. We are a long way from each other, but like they say, 'Absence makes the heart grow fonder.'"

An hour later, Anthony reread his letter to Judy he had just finished, signed it, "Love ya, Anthony," and addressed the envelope. He paused and realized he needed to get some postage stamps, so he set the letter on the bookshelf next to the photo of Judy—sort of an offering of commitment to his girlfriend so far away.

Observing all of this was Don, who was now hopping on one foot as he tried to put on his pants.

"Come on man, let's go have breakfast," Don suggested. The two of them headed to the dining hall in the Forest Fern Complex. While Anthony's high school cafeteria was made fun of for the quality of its food, the dining hall up here was renowned for its excellent cuisine. As they headed down the sunny path from the dorms to the dining hall, Anthony felt the crispness in the air and smelled the faint pine scent of the nearby trees.

Walking through the dining hall, which was filled with tables, they went through the doorway to the cafeteria line. Inside, they grabbed trays and silverware. Anthony had a made-to-order omelet by a guy wearing a white cook's jacket and a hairnet. His nametag said, "Buzz." Anthony filled a juice glass with fresh squeezed orange juice and put a piece of bread on the tractor-drive of an industrial quality toaster. The bread disappeared up into the machine and a minute later a piece of toast slid down the escape chute at the bottom of it. Don was waiting on another stainless-steel tray of pancakes to be delivered from the back kitchen.

Finding an empty table in the dining hall, they devoured their meals and contemplated going back for seconds, but decided they were actually quite full from their first serving. Don suggested taking a longer walk back to the dorms by way of a trail through the forest that surrounded the campus on its east side.

They descended several flights of steps and walked through a parking lot for some on-campus apartments. At the end of the parking lot was the trailhead for several trail loops through the forest. One hundred yards up the trail, and everything was changed. The bright rising sun was now blocked and filtered by redwood tree trunks and the coniferous foliage of the canopy. Only occasional thin shafts of light made its way to the forest floor where ferns drank up the dew dripping from the taller trees. The hard dirt trail at the edge of the parking lot had become a soft path, cushioned by pine needles—its comfort, inviting hikers deeper still into the primeval mist. The slight whiffs of pine scent that Anthony smelled on the way to the dining hall now gave way to an over-whelming pine aroma that filled his lungs. At one point, when Anthony and Don were far enough down the trail to be completely out of sight of the campus, they both stopped and gazed upward at the cathedral of the tallest trees on the planet. The slight breeze could be heard blowing gently through the treetops. He looked farther up the trail as it disappeared in a maze of redwood tree trunks. It was as if time didn't exist here—a place where one could see into eternity. Anthony could feel the spirits of nature behind every rock and tree.

Back at home in Southern California, Anthony's exposure to tall trees was pretty much limited to those in public botanical gardens—or as Joni Mitchell had called them, "tree museums." For the first time, Anthony got a glimpse of what others had told him as to why this place was so special. It was nature as God intended it to be. Once people experience the beauty of walking through a pristine forest—and see it, and smell it, and hear it; they are changed forever.

On Tuesday, in the second week of school, Anthony got out of his Marketing class at 10 a.m. There was a three-hour break in his schedule until his 1 p.m. Art History class. He walked across campus with a self-assured stride now that he had become familiar with his surroundings. He bounded through the outer door of the dorm and took the stairs two at a time heading up to his room on the third floor. He passed someone in the stairwell going down but didn't realize who it was until he stepped on to the third-floor landing.

"How'd it go?" Water Glass Girl's voice echoed in the concrete stairwell as she turned back to look up at him.

"What?"

"How'd it go?"

"How'd what go?"

"Your laundry. How'd your laundry turn out?"

"Everything is a shade of grey but it's clean. Thanks for asking."

Her dark eyes sparkled in an Audrey Hepburn-like way as she giggled at him.

"Good," she said smiling as she disappeared around the turn in the stairwell.

And she was gone.

Still staring where she had been, Anthony said to himself, *What's your name? What's your name? What's your name? Why is that so hard to say!*

Turning the corner into his hallway, he bumped into Keisha who had just been visiting with Randall.

"Hey Keisha, what's that girl's name that went to dinner with us that first night?"

"Child, there were a bunch of girls that went to dinner with us that night—and I didn't see you talking to none of them for very long, so I don't know who you be talkin' about," her one eyebrow raised in an accusing manner. Keisha seemed to be able to slide into and out of a black dialect any time she wanted.

"The one who hip-checked Randall."

"Ah, her! She's so sweet. If I be gay, I be all around her, but she's taken. Gotta nice white-boy back home. You out a luck, latecomer."

"Well, what's her name?"

"Susie-Mary or Mary-Sue somethin'. I don' know." Getting agitated, she added, "I gotta get to class. I ain't got time fo' no loser." And she too disappeared down the stairwell.

With most of the students taking a minimum full-time schedule (12 units) of classes for the first semester, there was plenty of free time to enjoy activities. No one had a lot of extra money to spend on activities however, so being a rather intelligent group, inventive games were made up on the spot. One of the early diversions was mattress rugby where they would stand a mattress up in the rather narrow dorm hallway and guys would hurl themselves against it trying to push it to the end of the hallway for a score. Guys on the other side of the mattress would be trying to push in the opposite direction. While no one ever scored, a lot of excess energy was used up while playing it. A score of 1-0 would have been a high scoring game.

Anthony joined in the ruckus and was crashing into the mattress, helping to push it a few feet down the hall. The back-and-forth stalemate eventually ended when all the participants were too exhausted to continue. A few guys lay against the fallen mattress as they caught their breath. The others returned to their rooms. Some headed straight for the showers. As Anthony turned to walk back to his room, a small group of girls had gathered at the hallway door to watch the sporting spectacle. They too were starting to disperse when Water Glass Girl stepped forward to a profusely sweaty Anthony and said, "Mary Sue. My name is Mary Sue Chandler." And with that, she spun on her heels and walked away.

The impromptu rugby games continued periodically over the next few months, but a stop was finally put to all rugby games when one of the unfortunate casualties was the drinking fountain in the middle of the hallway that someone caromed off of and broke the pipe, which flooded a poor girl's room below on second floor and ruined her semester art project. It was a picture of the Mona Lisa...made with dryer lint. Tragic. The girl was so distraught that her art project was ruined that she left school at the semester. Sequoia State University is a great place, but it's not for everybody. A collection was taken up to pay for the water damage. The girl's artwork, like the original, was irreplaceable.

CHAPTER 5
The People You Meet

The LGAs held occasional social activities during the first few weeks of school. It helped the dorm residents get to know each other and feel more at home. Anthony was meeting a growing number of people, although he wasn't sure about everybody's name—like the guy in the room next door. He had long hair and would play ZZ Top albums until late at night. Anthony would knock on his door and ask him to turn it down if it was a school night, and he was cool with that. If it was a Friday or Saturday, Anthony let him play the music as late as he wanted. This is what life is like in the dorms.

Then there was the dorm guru. Some guy named Vance. Keisha told Randall, who told Don that some students would seek him out for advice. Vance would play a song from an album and the lyrics would contain the answer.

No one ever saw Vance attend one class the entire time he lived in the dorms. His dorm room smelled of the pungent aroma of strawberry incense—which overpowered the sweet scent of cannabis. The room was dark. A large piece of fabric with a tapestry print on it covered the window. No one knew Vance's last name, although the rumor was that he was from Berkley—or Haight-Ashbury—or Santa Cruz.

Troubled students would knock on Vance's door seeking help for relationships, roommate problems, and general "meaning of life" conundrums. Vance would be sitting in a wicker chair at the far end of the small room; wearing blue jeans so faded, they almost looked white. His long dark hair hung down past his shoulders and onto the tie-dyed tank top that he was usually wearing.

Without speaking he would gesture for the visiting pilgrim to sit on the edge of the bed. On the wall above the bed hung a poster of Carlos Santana with one corner curled and hanging loose. From under eyelashes so long that it made the girls jealous, his eyes were crystal clear and he would listen intently to what the student was saying—nodding occasionally, sometimes shaking his head as if he felt the student's pain, sometimes smiling at a humorous comment. Never once during the monologue would Vance do anything to distract him from listening—and he'd never look away.

When the supplicant was finished, Vance would close his eyes as if he were trying to see into the soul of student—trying to find the correct prescription to ease the pain. After a few minutes, he would slowly stand and wander around the dark room, looking in one of the many dairy crates or cardboard boxes with record albums that filled most of the floor space left in the room besides the one bed, his whicker throne and the beanbag chair. He'd finger through the albums and then pull out one of the cardboard album covers. The song lyrics were not always clear, but many students read the lyrics written on the back of the album cover while listening to the music. With that and the residual cannabis vapor, the student would come away, if not completely enlightened, at least somewhat mollified and happy there was someone who would listen.

The girls' LGA on the third floor was a girl named Anita. She had a lot of patience, which she needed to put up with all of the drama that occurs in the dorms. Because the girls and guys dorms shared each floor, she not only had to deal with all her girls, she also had to deal with some of the guys that would venture into the girls' part of the dorms. Later in the year, she was a student teacher on an Indian reservation near SSU. That was probably a much easier assignment than being an LGA in the dorm. She was also a good friend of Mary Sue.

Some of the guys Anthony was getting to know were pretty good fishermen. They would come back with salmon and cook it in the little kitchen just off the first-floor lounge. One time, they went crabbing down on the wharf and Anthony went along with them. This Hispanic guy named Hector, from East L.A., showed him how to bait the traps (they looked like wire pyramids that were open flat). He'd put a piece of dead fish in the middle of the trap and then throw it over the side. They'd drink a beer and then pull up the trap. When they pull it up on to the wharf, it would be full of crabs hanging on the bars trying to escape. When Hector put the trap down on the deck, it opened, and the crabs started crawling every which way. Anthony almost jumped in the water to escape the little rascals. Hector knew which ones were legal to take and how big they had to be. He sorted through them and then cast out the trap a few more times. Hector took the crabs back to the dorms, cooked them in the little kitchen and had a crab feast like no one had ever seen. He fed everyone in the dorms until they were full and couldn't eat any more.

CHAPTER 6
Go Ask Vance

<u>October 1974</u>

Anthony was lying on his bed staring at the ceiling.

"Looks like you're not getting a lot of homework done there Bro," Don said as he entered their room.

"I am totally messed up."

"You're on something!"

"Not that kind of messed up. Confused messed up. I just got off the phone with Judy and all I can think about is that I want to ask Mary Sue out on a date. How messed up is that?"

"Wow dude, that IS messed up. You're a real low life."

"Hey, you're my roommate. You're supposed to back me up and tell me what to do!"

"Okay, okay. You gotta go to Vance. He'll help you, Bro."

"Don't tell me you've gone to see him before."

"No. But I have hung out with him before and he's pretty trippy."

Getting up off the bed, Anthony headed over to see Vance. He remembered that Randall had told him a little bit about Vance. In his mind he was thinking, *What can this...pothead say that will help me?*

Almost at the end of the hallway, Anthony stopped by a door on the left that had a psychedelic poster on it. He went to knock three times, but the door seemed to open by itself between the second and third knock. Vance was tending some houseplants under a grow-light. They sort of looked like False Aralia, but he wasn't sure. Maybe like the leaf on the helmet stickers of the Ohio State football team.

"Uh, hey Vance. Uh, sorry to bother you."

A girl sleeping in the beanbag chair shifted her position and then was still. In a softer voice, Anthony continued, "Uh, I was wondering if I could talk to you."

Vance folded back a canvas sleeping bag on the unmade bed and gestured for Anthony to sit. Then taking his seat in the wicker chair, he motioned for Anthony to speak.

"Well, I have this girl back home." He smelled the pungent smell of something burning in an ashtray on Vance's bookshelf. "Her name is..." *that smell is kind of sweet.* "Uh, her name is, uh...Judy. Yes, it is definitely Judy. And this other girl up here at school, her name is uh, Mary Lou... I mean Mary Sue." He wondered what was happening to his brain. The air was thick in this room, but he was okay, he thought. "And I just don't know what to do. You know what I mean?"

Vance smiled knowingly, nodding slowly as if he was absorbing not only Anthony's words, but also his feelings. Then he furrowed his brow as if he was looking at a horizon far beyond the walls of his dorm room. He was searching for the answer to this pilgrim's predicament. He seemed to be perplexed as he got up and paced back and forth between countless dairy crates, orange crates and cardboard boxes full of record albums. He went to reach for one, then stopped, then to another, and then paused again. Finally, it was if an ethereal light had come on. He bent down, moved two boxes and reached under a table pulling out a smaller box of seven-inch, 45 RPM single records. He shuffled through the first few then, in an "Ah ha" moment, pulled out the one for which he was looking. Reverently, like a priest handling a holy text, he removed the small vinyl disc from the paper cover. Going to his Pioneer Turntable, he made some adjustments, putting a plastic disk in the center of the larger hole in the vinyl record, and changing the speed of the turntable itself from 78 rpms to 45 rpms. The Marantz receiver and amp lit up as Vance brought his sound machine to life. He carefully lowered the needle and the twin Pioneer HPM-100 speakers crackled for a second, then the words to "If You Can't Be With the One You Love, Love the One You're With" from Stephen Stills' eponymous single from 1970 filled the room.

As the song played on, the girl in the beanbag chair shifted only slightly in her slumber. Anthony listened carefully to Still's lyrics. He felt that his eyes were squinting even though the light is Vance's room was very low, emanating from a three-wick sand candle on the small table.

When the song ended, the speakers crackled a bit again until Vance lifted the needle like a skilled surgeon. Anthony stood up and for no apparent reason, slightly bowed towards Vance. Showing Anthony towards the door, Vance had a tranquil look on his face that seemed to say, "Go in peace." At least that is what Anthony thought it meant. Vance closed the door and made a mental note that the next time he went to town, he had to get the "4-Way Street" album so he would have Stephen Stills' song on a 78 rpm album.

Anthony glided through the open door of his dorm room where Don was studying and plopped on the bed.

"Don, I'm asking her out!" exclaimed Anthony.

———————

Anthony figured that by this late on a Friday afternoon, all the girls in the girls' wing would be socializing. Doors would be open, animated conversations would be going on, music would be playing, laughter would be heard.

He was on a mission. He was looking for Mary Sue. As he walked from the boys' wing into the girls' hallway, he felt very nervous. His legs felt heavy and he had to think about every step he was taking. His arms did not seem to swing in rhythm with his stride. One girl, sitting cross-legged on the hallway floor with a small group of people looked up and said, "I know, John Wayne. You're imitating John Wayne."

Jeff, the LGA who was sitting in the group with Anita, the girls' LGA said, "That's a great idea for our next social get together. We'll have people imitate movie stars!" Anita loved the idea and they went on to discuss the details with the group. Anthony murmured something inaudible and moved awkwardly on looking for Mary Sue.

In the second dorm room from the end of the hallway, Mary Sue was standing in a doorway talking to two other girls in the room. Anthony walked up and waited for a lull in their conversation. Finally, Mary Sue turned towards Anthony, waiting for him to say something. As Anthony gazed at her, he literally got lost in the dark pools of her eyes. The top button of her flannel shirt was unbuttoned revealing her soft smooth neck and throat. She leaned casually against the door jam and cocked her head a little to the side as if to say, "Yes?"

Anthony, tried to swallow, but he had no saliva. His tongue was stuck to the roof of his completely dry mouth. He tried to strike a cool pose, but it looked more like a spastic involuntary movement. Finally, he stammered out a sentence that contained the words: "Saturday," "movies," and "go."

Mary Sue smiled and said, "Sure."

Nodding, he turned and "John Wayne" stiffly walked the length of the girls' hallway, oblivious to the laughter, music, and antics of the people around him.

Mary turned to the girls in the room and made big eyes and put her hand over her open mouth as if to stifle a laugh. Then all the girls giggled gleefully.

As he turned into the boys' wing, Anthony thought to himself, *I sure wish that girl was a better conversationalist.*

CHAPTER 7
The Date

"Don't worry about it! You got it made in the shade. A movie is a great first date. You don't have to say shit. Trust me. You just make small talk walking to the theater, then you got about two hours of just watching the movie, and then you walk her home. Piece of cake." Don's comments seemed sound, and his advice to see Vance proved to work out the other day. Maybe Anthony could get through this date after all.

––––––––––––––

The next morning, everyone seemed to know about "The Date". That's how things worked in the dorms. And that is why most people eventually moved out of the dorms. There was very little privacy.

Anthony walked down the hallway when he heard someone singing, "And they called it Puppy Love." It was Tyrone, the basketball player from Watts whose room was near the water fountain in the middle of the hallway. He was serenading Anthony as others poked their heads out of their rooms grinning and wishing Anthony good luck on his date that evening.

Hector walked out of his room and sort of got into Anthony's face and said, "Hey gringo, Maria Sue is like my Hermana. You be nice to her." Anthony wasn't sure if he was joking or not, but owing to his smaller size and milder disposition, he figured he better not piss off the larger and more agitated Hector.

By the time Anthony got to the end of the hallway, literally everyone had their door opened and were clapping for him. He was a bit of a celebrity because he had the nerve to ask Mary Sue out on a date.

HECTOR SPEAKING TO THE READER...

"You know, Maria Sue is about the nicest person in the dorms. Everyone likes her. I am not sure, I don't know, but I think it has something to do with the fact that she treats everyone with respect. In the Chicano culture, respect is very important. I have seen her be friendly with the most popular people in our dorm, like Randall. Then I will see her be nice to that geeky chick with the big glasses that is always carrying a stack of books that weigh as much as she does. Maria Sue will even help her carry some of those books up the stairs to her room. I'm not sure what is going on with Maria Sue's boyfriend back home. I hear they are serious. But I REALLY don't get what she sees in Anthony. I mean, he is nice enough, but...I just don't see it happening. Plus, if he tries anything, I am gonna kick his gringo ass. I am. I really am."

———————

Late Saturday afternoon, Anthony headed to the cafeteria for a quick dinner and his new favorite dessert, vanilla ice cream from the soft-serve ice cream machine. He ate light, except for the ice cream since he was more than a bit nervous. Nervous about going out with Mary Sue and nervous about Hector threatening him. After he ate, he headed for the showers and then got dressed. Corduroy pants, placket-collared shirt, windbreaker.

He opened his door and walked into the girls' wing. Only a few people were milling about and Anthony was not as nervous or stiff-legged as he was the day before. Maybe it was because he wasn't worried about being rejected at this point. Mary Sue had agreed to go out on the date. He might get rejected at some point in the future, but for the moment, things were good.

He knocked on Mary's door and she opened it promptly. She was dressed in a white, long-sleeve western style blouse, and Lee's blue jeans and carried a grey-blue bulky knit sweater. Anthony could tell she was now wearing some eye make-up although she really didn't need it. They walked down the hall together as a few people looked on and smiled. He opened the door and they descended the stairs, went out the door and started walking into town.

"So, Anthony...or do people call you 'Antonio'? Where're you from?"

"'Never been called Antonio. I'm from Southern California."

"Ah, near Disneyland? I have a friend who lives near it."

"Uh, no. It's funny how people associate all of SoCal with Disneyland. I mean it is there, but Southern California doesn't revolve around Cinderella's Castle. How about you? Let me see, I hear you have two first names. You must be special. My mom only gave me one first name."

"No-ah," she said making the word "no" into a two-syllable word for emphasis. Smiling at his wit, she continued, "Mary is my first name. Susan is my middle name. Actually, Susan is the name of my maternal grandmother."

"And you are from...?"

"Well, smart guy, what have you heard about that?"

"You are from a town in the Wenatchee Valley in Washington state, where your boyfriend lives."

What the heck are you thinking, Anthony thought to himself. *Well, better to address this now and get it out in the open.*

She wasn't smiling at his wit now. The sparkle was gone from her dark eyes.

"Yes," she said looking away. "My father is a farmer and we live near Hilland."

"Hilland—in the Wenatchee 'Valley'? Isn't that a bit of a misnomer? Are their any hills in Hilland?"

Careful big guy, there is being witty and there is being a smart-ass, Anthony scolded himself. *You are coming very close to the later.*

"Hilland is not named for any hills. It is named for the first resident and the town's founder, Abner Hilland."

"Like, is there a statue of ole' Abner in the town square?"

"LIKE no-ah." Two syllables again. "We don't have a town square. By the way, is that a photo of your sweet sister on your bookshelf in your room?" she questioned with one eyebrow raised. She put particular emphasis on the word "sister."

Touché, Anthony thought. This girl had apparently done a little homework of her own.

They took a few more steps in silence and Anthony sort of let her question blow away on the cool fall breeze that blew up some dead leaves on the sidewalk near the theater. He figured it was a rhetorical question and that she wasn't really asking a question but was just letting him know that she knew as much about him as he knew about her. Not only was this girl pretty, but she was also smart.

At the ticket window, Anthony laid down a five-dollar bill and collected two tickets. He let Mary go in first, then handed the two tickets to the same guy who had just sold him the tickets. He had walked out of the booth and was now standing by the door. Looking at his red military-style usher's coat, Anthony said, "If I don't make it out alive, take the rest of the troops and report back to Lieutenant Hanley," a reference to Rick Jason's character in the "Combat" series, one of Anthony's favorites TV shows while growing up. Anthony cracked up at his own joke. The usher looked unamused. Mary Sue raised that eyebrow again.

They sat in two of the red velvet chairs (red seemed to be the predominant color in the place) in the center of the theatre. A few people sat here and there, and a few more shuffled in before the lights dimmed and the previews of coming attractions began. After that and the reminder to visit the refreshment stand, Anthony remembered that he had bought two candy bars from the vending machine in the lounge of the dorms. He offered one to Mary Sue, which she accepted—somewhat touched by his thoughtfulness.

"Now what kind of wine should I have brought to go with our candy bars," Anthony said, trying to make small talk before the movie started.

"There is only one wine," she replied.

"Boone Farm Strawberry Hill?" he teased.

"Why? Cuz I live on a farm?" she said making a face at him. "I am a Chablis Girl. Classy and light but not too sweet."

"I'll vouch for that," he said regretting it as soon as it came out of his mouth.

"Is this movie going to start soon?" she asked somewhat annoyed.

Soon the feature attraction appeared on the screen and Anthony exhaled and sank back into the chair and the surrounding darkness. Things were not going as well as Don had predicted, but at least he was right in that Anthony now had ninety minutes or so where he didn't need to talk at all. At least he couldn't get in too much trouble while sitting quietly in a theatre.

There was however the social challenges of sitting next to someone on a first date. After the spirited exchange on the walk down to the theatre, Anthony figured things were a little icy at the moment. He carefully positioned his right leg (the one closest to her) straight ahead so as to not have any contact with her left leg. He then positioned his right arm on the shared armrest at the forward most part so she could rest her elbow on the same armrest closer to the back cushion of the chair.

What was this movie about? Anthony thought to himself as he negotiated the social gymnastics of this awkward situation. He glanced sideways and saw that Mary was casually munching on the proffered candy bar and seemed to be intrigued by the storyline of the movie.

Later in the movie, apparently some kind of romance-comedy, something funny happened on the screen and Mary Sue laughed and leaned slightly against Anthony's arm as if she was sharing the funny moment with him. Anthony was a bit taken back by this show of physical affection. Okay, maybe it wasn't all that, but it was certainly a surprise to Anthony.

The sun was down and the wind blew colder as they walked back to the dorms after the movie. As if calling a truce, the conversation stayed light and superficial, mainly focused on the various subplots and characters in the movie. At one point Anthony put his hands on Mary Sue's arms from a step behind her and moved her to the other side of the sidewalk—somewhat startling her. "I'll block the wind for you," he answered before she could ask the question. She tucked her chin into the thick collar of her sweater and smiled.

Retracing their way up the dorm stairs to the third floor, Anthony walked Mary Sue to her room. She turned and holding both of his hands in hers, said, "I had a wonderful time tonight. Thank you. Let's talk about the people at home another time."

"Okay," was all that he said.

And with that she turned her head slightly, leaned closer and kissed him gently on the lips. "Good night Antonio," adding a comical accent to "Antonio."

"Good night Chablis Girl," he replied.

Then she walked into her room closing the door behind her.

Anthony walked down the hallway back towards his room, still not sure what to think of the evening's events.

At the end of the hall, he passed the slightly plump girl coming in the opposite direction. He smiled and said, "Hey!" She smiled and nodded back at him. Anthony felt that he had made progress in reaching out to this isolated person.

As the girl passed Anthony, she shook her head and wondered what he saw in Mary Sue. He could do much better, she thought.

———————

Upon entering his hallway, Anthony bumped into Tyrone who was walking down the hall the other way and again he sang out, "They call it Puppy Love." He actually had a good voice and sounded a bit like Paul Anka.

Don was standing outside their room talking to a few guys as Anthony walked up. "Well, how'd it go?" one of them asked.

"Did you kiss her?" Don asked.

"Yeah, yeah, did you get a good night kiss?" another said.

"Sure," Anthony said self-assuredly, acting as cool as the others expected him to be after having kissed Mary Sue. It was like he now had celebrity status among the guys on third floor.

"Ah, you!" one of the guys said admiringly.

Anthony smiled to the crowd, and then gave a cautious glance up the hallway towards Hector's room. The door was closed. Everything was great. Anthony excused himself, entered his room and had the best night's sleep since he had arrived at Sequoia State.

CHAPTER 8
Crash and Burn

The next morning being Sunday, everyone slept in a bit. Don was actually the first one up and had gone down the hall to the restroom when Anthony woke up. *It is a beautiful day,* he thought to himself. When Don returned, he said, "You old dog! Everyone is talking about you."

More levelheaded now than last night, Anthony said, "It's really no big deal. She still has a boyfriend back home and I still have Judy."

Anthony got dressed and together he and Don headed down to have a late breakfast. On the way down the stairs, they passed Shelley, who happened to be Mary Sue's roommate. She had long dark hair and looked a bit like Cher. Anthony smiled and Don said a friendly "Hi" to Shelley. However, Shelley returned their greeting by shaking her head side to side and said, "You should never kiss and tell." With that, she passed them without smiling.

"What's up with that?" Don asked out loud.

"I don't know," answered Anthony. But deep down, he had a feeling, and it wasn't good.

In the dining hall, as Don and Anthony were in line holding their cafeteria trays, from behind the steel counter and glass partition, Buzz gave Anthony a big thumbs up. *Okay, this is going too far,* Anthony thought to himself. He certainly did not want all this notoriety, although he did nothing to cool it last night.

When Dan and Anthony got their trays filled with the Sunday morning faire, they looked for an open table at which to sit. As they were surveying the dining room, Anthony saw Anita in deep conversation with Hector. As Don and Anthony walked by, Anita scowled at him and Hector glared. *Oh shit. Something has gone terribly wrong,* Anthony thought to himself. As Don sat down to eat, Anthony left his tray on the table and burst out of the dining hall, sprinting up the path to the dorms. Inside, he took the stairs two at a time until he reached the third floor. Walking now and trying to catch his breath, he turned into the girls' hallway towards Mary Sue's room. Near the opposite end of the hallway, he saw her—and she saw him. She was just coming from the girls' showers and was wearing a white robe and had her hair up in a towel. She wore no make-up. She still looked great, except for the fact that she looked madder than Anita and Hector combined. Anthony walked quickly towards her to explain and she was walking towards him at an equal pace. People in the hallway were throwing themselves against the walls to stay out of the way of the two trains on a collision course. Of course, everyone getting out of the way had their backs to the wall because they wanted to see the impending explosion that would certainly be the most excitement in the dorms so far this school year.

10 feet away—Mary Sue was shooting lasers through her eyes at him.
7 feet away—Anthony thought she looked hot...in more ways than one.
3 feet away—Mary Sue's jaws were clenched shut in total anger.
1 foot away—Anthony said, "Let me explain."

Grabbing Anthony by the arm of his jacket, not unlike an elementary school teacher would when she would escort a bad student to the principal's office, she shoved him through an open door into the slightly plump girl's room. She was studying at her desk against

the wall and was stunned to see these two people,
whom she hardly knew, burst into her ordinarily quiet
space.

Mary Sue released her grip on Anthony's jacket
and slammed the door shut. The people in the hallway
gave a collective sigh of disappointment, and then
returned to their conversations as if nothing had
happened.

"I am so mad at you," Mary Sue began. "We had a
nice time last night and I thought you were kind of a
good guy, ...the candy bar, ...the blocking the wind for
me. THAT'S why I kissed you last night. I did NOT
expect that this morning, EVERYONE in the damn dorm
would know that we kissed. Especially since I told NO
ONE!"

The plump girl, still frozen at her desk, watched
and listened intently.

"I have never been so humiliated in all my life,"
she stated emphatically as if they were the only two
people in the room.

Anthony had three images pass through his head
in quick succession—the Hindenburg crashing at
Lakehurst NAS, an atomic explosion at the Alamogordo
nuclear testing ground, and the town of Atlanta going
up in flames in the movie, "Gone with the Wind."

"Please let me explain," Anthony stammered, still
not believing he had such a great date last night, but
today it was all ruined. Then he saw tears coming down
Mary Sue's cheeks as she looked down. That crushed
him. To this point, he was afraid of her anger, but as
angry as she was, it was nothing compared to the anger
sometimes shown by his high school football coaches.
But now he saw that his behavior had hurt her deeply
and that took all of the air out of him.

Speaking softly, his voice barely audible, he continued, "I had a great time too. I really did." Not really knowing where he was going with this, he paused for a moment. Then he switched his tone from an absolute apology to a calmer, more logical approach as to what really happened.

"Mary Sue, whether you know it or not, you are thought of as a really nice person by everyone in the dorm—by both the girls and the boys. The guys were just excited that we were going out together. They very innocently asked if I kissed you good night, that's all. I said, 'Yes.' I did NOT say we 'made out'. I did NOT say, 'we did IT'. Your reputation was not tarnished at all. Again, I am sorry. I will never, ever say anything like that again."

Mary Sue, still standing with her arms crossed seemed to absorb everything Anthony had said. *When you look at it like that, maybe it wasn't so bad*, she thought. She wiped her tears from her cheeks with the sleeve of her robe. Anthony leaned forward and gave her a consoling hug, which she accepted but did not reciprocate. When he released her, she nodded, opened the door, and walked back to her room.

Anthony exhaled deeply and walked out of the room a moment later. He did not know where he stood with her, but at least she did not seem outrageously mad at the moment. Then he realized he exercised some pretty quick thinking. *I wonder if I can still change my major to pre-law*, he thought.

The slightly plump girl, still frozen at her desk, stared at the open door and wondered what in the heck just happened.

CHAPTER 9
The Big Game

November 1974

For a while, things stayed kind of distant between Anthony and Mary Sue. A week after their date, two events were scheduled that would prove interesting. First, their dorm had been challenged to a football game by the rival dorm across the quad. No one knew why it was a rivalry, primarily because very few people stayed in the dorm for more than a year. Even still, the boys' wing of the dorm was excited for the chance to go out and burn some energy without the threat of breaking a water fountain or ruining a girl's art project.

The other event was that Mary Sue's boyfriend was coming down to school to visit her for the weekend. He arrived Friday evening.

The kick-off of "The Big Game" (Not to be confused with "The Big Game"—Cal vs. Stanford) was scheduled for Saturday at 10 a.m. Some of the guys who were playing in the game actually went to bed a bit early on Friday night—early being around midnight. The team, such as it was, all went to breakfast together in the dining hall early that morning. Back at the dorm, some players got dressed in old football jerseys they had from home—of course, none of them matched. Others wore old sweatshirts. Most wore jeans or sweatpants. A few guys who had played high school ball wore their old cleats, while the others wore tennis shoes. One guy wore hiking boots—a real fashion statement.

At 9:30 a.m., the motley bunch of players filed down the stairs and out of the dorm. At the same time, the rivals were coming out of their dorm. Behind both teams, a crowd of onlookers followed. Most wore jackets and a few brought blankets for protection from the cold, moist air. Some of the girls brought drinks and snacks to munch on during the game. The day started with a blue-grey November sky, but it was breaking up and the sun was starting to come through the clouds. Being a Saturday morning, there were very few people on campus, so the crowd of players and fans attracted some mild attention. One homeless guy, who was carrying on a conversation with himself as he sat on a bench on campus, saw the moving crowd. He had wandered on to the campus from hitchhiking on Highway 101. Joining the moving group, he did not know where they were headed or why.

Today's game will be played in California Memorial Stadium on the campus of the University of California at Berkeley—no wait. Wrong "Big Game."

Today's game will be played on the upper field behind the football stadium on the campus of Sequoia State University. In the fall, it serves as a practice field for the real Sequoia State football team. In the spring, it serves as the girls' softball field. Although it was not in the greatest shape, with the grass torn up and many bare spots, the field was clearly marked and lined.

The surroundings probably made that field one of the most beautiful football venues on the West Coast. On one side was the back of the home stands of the football stadium. In fact, the real football team would film their practices from atop the back of the stadium. The other three sides of the field were bordered with beautiful pine and redwood forests. No fence. No wall. No barrier of any kind. The edge of the grass just stopped, and the forest began. Rumor has it that once a softball player from a visiting team was chasing a foul ball and ran into the forest to retrieve it and was never seen again.

If Keith Jackson were introducing the game on television that morning, it would probably have sounded something like this...

> "When the cold November wind blows off the Pacific and through the redwood trees in the great northwest of California, most people stay inside by the warmth of a fire. However, a few hearty souls venture out into the elements to test their mettle against their rival dorm. Soon, their hot steaming breath will mix with the frosty chill of the forest air along the line of scrimmage before the clash of bodies starts the next play. Both teams hungry for a win, but only one team will emerge victorious. Rival Dorms. The Big Game. On the back field. Sit back and enjoy it folks—IT JUST DOESN'T GET ANY BETTER THAN THIS!"

Okay, so maybe that is what Keith Jackson <u>would</u> have said if the game had been televised, but he didn't and it isn't.

While both teams went through their informal stretching and warm-ups, the crowd of fans split up, each taking a sideline. There was practically a capacity crowd of 15 on each sideline, which included the homeless guy who stayed on the side with Keisha, Shelly, the slightly plump girl, Natalie and Lena, and Anita—primarily because they looked like they were carrying more food than the rival dorm's fans.

Although the plump girl had few friends up at school, she decided to tag along and watch the game—from a distance. Besides being a bit overweight, she was not particularly attractive and did little in the way of hairstyle or makeup to enhance her appearance. Being that way, she did not seek friendships because of previous rejections. So, it created a vicious cycle. The more she withdrew, the fewer friends she had, which caused her to withdraw further.

Anthony noticed her standing apart from the others on the sidelines and remembered that when he would pass her in the hallway, or on the stairs, or on campus; she would not even make eye contact. In her mind, if she made eye contact, she would feel compelled to say, "Hello," which might or might not be reciprocated. And that was a pain she had felt too often, so it was easier and safer to withdraw completely.

As Anthony was warming up with his teammates, he glanced over at her and smiled. After all, she came out to support the team. She smiled back, and that small gesture pulled her back from a cliff of her own making, completely unbeknownst to Anthony.

He made a mental note to greet her whenever they passed in the dorms or on campus. He didn't really know what was happening in the world, but was perceptive to the feelings of some people in his realm.

When Anthony's team huddled after the opening kick-off, all the guys with cleats played wide receivers, running backs, and quarterback. In the first series, Randall tried to throw a pass to Tyrone, but was sacked before he could get the ball away. Facing a long yardage situation, Randall threw a screen pass to Anthony. He had stepped behind the line of scrimmage, caught the quick pass and turned to run up field when he thought he had run into a brick wall. As he crashed to the ground, he saw stars, his nose burned and he couldn't breathe. With his blurry vision, he saw someone staring down at him and figured it was an opponent. When he was finally able to focus his eyes again, he saw it was Hector with whom he had collided during the play. Anthony reached up a hand for some help as he tried to stand. Hector just stared at him, then turned and walked back to the huddle. *Message received*, Anthony thought to himself. *Message received.*

In the next series the rivals had the ball and were putting the ball in the air. Flynn was trying to rush the quarterback while a guy named Igor blocked him. Igor was a big, burly guy with an unkempt beard, who always wore bib-overalls. He was their toughest, dirtiest player and tried to hurt people when he played the game. When Flynn was almost past him, Igor grabbed him and threw him to the ground—then body-slammed his 240 pounds on top of the diminutive Flynn who weighed about 130 pounds if he were dripping wet. It was a flagrant infraction of the rules as well as poor sportsmanship. The dorm sideline all booed furiously. Even the homeless guy, who had his face buried in a bag of potato chips that the Banshee Sisters had given him, yelled, "That's bullshit!" It was pretty blatant if the homeless guy could see it. Flynn lay motionless for a few moments before Hector extended a hand and helped him to his feet.

Two series later, Randall handed off to Jeff who ran to his left. Jeff then flipped the ball to Anthony who came behind him and was running to the right on a reverse. Hector who had faked a poor block against Igor, peeled back around. When Igor reacted to the reverse and changed directions, Hector, in a full sprint, hit him broadside as hard as he could. The hit made a sickening sound as both bodies collided. Hector had left his feet as he fully extended himself on contact into Igor's ribcage. Igor looked as though he had be shot by a high-powered rifle and crumpled to the ground.

As the play continued, Anthony, who was carrying the ball under his arm as he sprinted toward the right sideline, stopped suddenly and brought the ball up to throw. Tyrone, who had worked himself across the field and deep, was wide open and Anthony threw him the ball. Never breaking stride, Tyrone gathered in the ball and glided into the end zone for the score.

A small crowd of rival dorm players helped Igor off the field. It appeared that he might have cracked a rib. Hector just nodded and walked back to the huddle. "The Enforcer," someone said. *"Respect,"* Hector thought to himself.

The rivals were clearly the better team with many players bigger and faster than anyone on Anthony's team. They ended up falling behind the rivals later in the game although Anthony caught a nice pass from Randall in the corner of the end zone for a TD—with his feet dragging to stay inbounds. In true sophomoric fashion, he checked to make sure the girls from the dorm had seen the catch. He acted very cool, like he did that all the time. In his coolness, he scanned the crowd and saw Keisha, Shelly, the plump girl—who was now standing closer to the rest of the group, along with Natalie and Lena, Anita and the homeless guy on the sideline enjoying the game—but no Mary Sue or her boyfriend.

Late in the game and still behind in the score, they dejectedly walked back to the huddle. Don addressed the group, "I'm tired of this shit. Here's what we're going to do. Randall, you are the quarterback."

"I have been the quarterback the whole game," he pointed out.

"Shut up! All the guys with cleats are now playing offensive line. Flynn, you are the running back. Okay, the first play is Sweep right." Flynn was a quick guy, even though he was wearing hiking boots for the game. They gave him the ball four straight times while in the offensive line, Anthony, Don and Hector were pulling, and trapping and cross-blocking—and they started moving the ball down the field with gains of 6 yards, 9 yards, 4 yards, 11 yards.

Back in the huddle, Don said, "Now listen! This time Randall, fake it to Flynn on the Sweep right. I'll block down on your guy Bro. You pull and kick out the left defensive end. Hector, you pull from the right side and turn up field and Randall you follow him. And Flynn, carry out your fake and make someone tackle you." Flynn nodded. The play started just as the previous four plays had started with Randall reaching forward to hand Flynn the ball. Randall rode him and at the last second, pulled the ball from Flynn, who was quickly tackled by three or four defenders. By now, Hector who showed amazing speed and agility for a guy who was a midnight snack away from 260 lbs., was coming across from his right tackle position and turned up in the hole created by Don and Anthony on the left side of the line. Randall was right behind him. Hector, at a full sprint now, knocked down a linebacker, then shoved a defensive back to the ground. The safety came over to try to make the tackle, but Randall slid to the left between Hector and the sideline. Hector merely shielded him from the safety and Randall sprinted untouched the last thirty yards for the score.

Both still sprawled on the ground from their blocks, Don nodded at Anthony and Anthony knew exactly what Don meant. The fans went wild.

The next series the rival dorm tried a long pass and Tyrone made a one-handed interception. He raced untouched down the far sidelines for another quick touchdown. Most of the fans were cheering on the sideline except for Natalie and Lena. They were booing.

Don yelled at them, "What are you doing? We just scored two in a row and you're booing?"

"We feel sorry for the other team," they protested.

"THEY ARE STILL AHEAD BY TWO TOUCHDOWNS! Go sit on the other side if you are going to cheer for them!" Don said in disgust.

The Banshee Sisters stood defiantly, arm in arm and proclaimed, "We can stand wherever we want." An out-of-breath Tyrone jogged up with the ball and a confused look on his face as he surveyed the argument on the sideline.

The game continued but exhaustion was setting in and the enthusiasm seemed to be waning on both sides. There was no further scoring and finally the game was called. The rivals celebrated what they said was their thirty-first consecutive victory in the annual match up of "The Big Game"—which is a bit odd since the two dorms on either side of the quad were only built ten years ago.

The fans packed up their snacks and trash. The homeless guy asked if he could have a schedule of future games. The players from both sides shook hands, except for Igor who had returned to his dorm a half hour ago, still holding his side. The crowd and players filed down the path along the football stadium and on to the center of campus on their way back to the dorms.

———————

Even though they lost, the dorm had a party that night. Everyone from all three floors congregated in the first-floor lounge screaming in conversation so as to be heard above the loud music. Most had something to drink and all were having a good time, while some were nursing some pretty bad bruises and cuts. Anthony sat on the sofa, talking to some people from first floor who were also from Southern California. As he looked around the room, he saw the plump girl talking to some other girls, which he was happy to see. He also caught Natalie looking at him. When their eyes met, Natalie smiled coyly and looked away—her eyebrows raised as if to say, "No, you didn't see me looking at you."

That was interesting and unexpected, Anthony thought to himself. He got up from the sofa to refill his drink and as he stood, he was face to face with Hector.

"Nice catch," was all he said. Anthony held his breath as Hector turned and walked away. Walking toward the drink table, he scanned the whole room but did not see Mary Sue or her boyfriend.

Finally, late into the night, the party ended and people drifted back upstairs to their rooms. Anthony and Don walked up the stairs slowly like two old men as they nursed their wounds from the game. Anthony didn't even look down the girls' hallway as he turned the corner toward his room.

The last thing Anthony heard before he drifted off the sleep that night was Don saying, "Good game Bro."

CHAPTER 10
A Second Chance

Monday morning, Anthony was sitting in his Business Communications class listening to the professor lecture about the elements of the Communication Model.

'The message travels from the sender to the receiver, but as it travels, it passes through filters. What are some of the filters that the message might pass through that would detract from the message?"

"Noise?"

"Good. Yes physical noise is one of the most obvious filters. How about another?"

"Frame of mind?"

"Good. The frame of mind of the receiver can quite distort the message that is sent. How about another...

I wonder what happened with Mary Sue and her boyfriend this past weekend, Anthony thought to himself. *I wonder if she told him about me? Well, you certainly haven't told Judy about her!* He sighed deeply and looked at the clock on the wall. Forty more minutes were left until the end of class. *Cheese and crackers, won't this guy ever stop lecturing?*

Finally, class ended and Anthony strolled across campus towards the Forest Fern Complex to check his mail. In the middle of campus, there were posters supporting many different causes. A few people were sitting at card tables, passing out pamphlets with information on saving the Spotted Owl, or renewable energy, or freeing Tibet. Anthony wondered who was keeping Tibet from being free. He made a mental note to find out and to be more aware of what was happening in the world, although his world seemed to be in chaos right now.

He could see something through the little window of the post office box style mailbox. Turning the key, he opened the metal door and pulled out an envelope from Judy. He opened it quickly and took out a Ziggy greeting card with a sad-faced Ziggy on the front. On the inside, the message said something about missing you. Judy had written a note on the back saying how well school was going but that things seemed different with Anthony's class now graduated and gone. She also said that Tim, Anthony's friend and teammate from last year who was going to Southwestern State U., had stopped by and said to say hello. Anthony returned to his room and put the card on the bookshelf next to Judy's photo and lay back on the bed with his hands behind his head, considering his destiny.

As Anthony was lost in thought, he felt the cool breeze blowing in through his window. By leaving his door open, the breeze blew in efficiently from one end of the room to the other. Then, to his surprise, coming through the door was Mary Sue.

Not knowing what to say, Anthony waited for her to open the conversation.

"I know I got upset at you the other day, Antonio," again adding a comical accent to "Antonio."

Anthony again pictured the Hindenburg bursting into flames.

"I have a lot on my mind besides school right now," she continued. "I talked to Jim about some things this weekend," the rest of her sentence fading in the breeze coming through the window.

"So, Jim is your sweet brother?" Anthony asked sarcastically. He immediately wished he hadn't said it.

She squinted at him and with an admonishing look on her face.

"No-ah," again, two syllables for emphasis. "He's my boyfriend. Jim Martin. He's a few years older than me. We grew up in Hilland. Went to the same schools. He is an apple farmer now. 'Has his own farm. Or he will when he inherits his dad's farm. He wants to expand soon by leasing land from other farmers."

"Just like your dad, I am guessing?"

"Pretty much." She was pacing back and forth in the room while Anthony was propped up on one elbow, still on his bed. She paused and looked at Judy's photo on the bookshelf. "So, who is this?"

"That's Judy."

"And she is your...?" a long pause while waiting for an answer.

"Girlfriend—for two years now and counting. She is a year behind me in school. She's thinking of enrolling here next year after she graduates."

"Well, won't that be interesting," she said sarcastically.

Another long pause.

"So Mary, what are we doing here?" Anthony asked assertively—not the way he usually acted.

"What do you mean?" although she knew exactly what he meant.

"You know, you and me. I think there is a little chemistry between us. Am I wrong?"

"No, you're not wrong," she said, but could not look at him as she said it.

"So what do we do?" he asked.

"So what do we do?" she asked.

Another long pause.

"You know, I'm new at figuring out big feelings," he stated.

Mary continued, "Me too. I feel like I am trying to find my destiny. My <u>own</u> destiny."

"A wise man once told me, 'You don't find your destiny. Your destiny finds you.'"

She mulled that over in her mind and nodded slowly. "How about we go for a walk after dinner one night this week?"

"Love to," he said with an economy of words.

"Good," she replied and then left the room. Then leaning back, she popped her head inside and said, "How about Wednesday night?"

"Can't—night class. How about Thursday?"

"Done," she replied. Then she disappeared.

Then she leaned back through the doorway again and said, "And if you tell anyone…" Her voice trailed off and she gave him a dirty look. He feigned a fearful look. She disappeared again going down the hall in one direction as Hector walked by going in the other direction. Anthony's fearful look was not feigned this time.

CHAPTER 11
Guess Who's Coming to Thanksgiving Dinner

On Wednesday, in the late afternoon, Anthony headed down for an early dinner before his evening Astronomy class. After dinner, he went back for his usual favorite dessert of vanilla ice cream from the soft-serve ice cream machine. On the way back to his table, he noticed other people enjoying a variety of ice cream favors. Thinking he had missed the other flavored machines, he walked back into the cafeteria area and looked all around. All he could see was the vanilla machine where he had filled his bowl. Coming back to the table, he approached Dylan, who was enjoying a bowl of chocolate ice cream.

"Okay, Dylan! Where's the chocolate ice cream machine? I looked all over!"

Laughing, Dylan walked Anthony over to the coffee bar that also served hot chocolate and picked up a packet of powdered hot chocolate. Tearing open the packet, he sprinkled it on Anthony's vanilla ice cream and took his spoon and stirred it until it was completely mixed.

"Viola! Chocolate ice cream. 'You want mocha ice cream? You use a packet of instant coffee. For chocolate-mocha, mix the chocolate powder and the instant coffee. For fruit flavors, take your vanilla ice cream over to the toaster area and put a spoonful of strawberry jam on it. Leave it as a topping or stir it into the ice cream. You can even make a banana split. Just peel and slice a banana from the fresh fruit basket at the beginning of the cafeteria line. We have a whole ice cream parlor in the dining hall; you just need to learn where to find it."

The things you learn in college, Anthony thought to himself.

"It is just like the salad bar," Dylan went on. The dining hall had a salad bar with a whole produce department of vegetables. There were two kinds of lettuce as well as fresh spinach plus toppings like mushrooms, sprouts, raisins, sliced carrots, bacon pieces, shredded cheese, sunflower seeds and fresh toasted croutons made from the previous days bread. There were three dressing choices—Italian, French, and Ranch.

"If you like Thousand Island dressing, you go to the condiment station and get a packet of ketchup, mayonnaise, and relish. Mix it all together and you have Thousand Island dressing!" Dylan instructed.

Sheer genius, Anthony thought in amazement.

Wednesday evening, Anthony stuck around after his Astronomy class to talk to the professor about an assignment that was soon due. The professor, with disheveled hair, a well-worn sport coat and a briefcase in one hand and a stack of astronomy books in another, answered the questions of several students including Anthony's before making his way back to his office. The old guy was nearing retirement, but still had a passion for his subject. The fact that students had questions after class seemed to energize him where some professors would be annoyed by the delay in getting out of the classroom door. This guy had found his destiny literally in the stars, and it gave him an inner peace that most people lacked.

Anthony, with questions answered, started across campus, walking back towards the dorm. As he passed the School of Music, he heard a pianist practicing "Fantasia in C Minor" by Joseph Haydn, a beautiful classical piece. It was almost surreal, as the crisp air of a November evening seemed to beckon the music to come outside and dance on the wind as it kicked up fall-colored leaves and spilled them across the campus. The piano music seemed to provide a soundtrack to Anthony's college experience at this moment in time.

He passed Don heading the opposite direction on his way to the library. They greeted briefly and without thinking, Anthony said, "I'll see you back home."

Wait, what? Anthony thought. *Where'd that come from?* "I'll see you back home." The words had just come out and no one was more surprised than Anthony.

"I'll see you back home." *When did that happen? When did that cold cinderblock building, which was painted that god-awful institutional beige, with its stained sofas, lumpy mattresses, and battered furniture— when did that become home?*

As he had done many times in the last month, Anthony looked up at the dorm building from a distance. It was still imposing, institutional and by now a fixture in Anthony's life and days. This evening though, he saw it with different eyes. He began walking toward it, and still a ways away, he heard it.

The dorm's walls and windows couldn't contain the multitude of different conversations, music and laughter. Each different sound somehow weaving together a harmonious and welcoming melody, not unlike the piano piece the student was practicing, which carried out of the building to Anthony's ears. The lights from the rooms cascaded out, casting a golden hue to the building as if it were glowing with a welcoming greeting.

Walking closer, he could make out through the open windows, the bustle of activity inside and the source of the building's sounds and song. Closer still,

Anthony could make out faces and he stopped short. Those inside had names he knew and laughs he recognized. No longer strangers, they were now his dorm mates, his classmates, and even more, his friends.

When Anthony had arrived in September, his was one nondescript room among many in one nondescript building on a campus of many. Now, as he reached for the door, he heard the building's song, felt its pulse and, as if for the first time, Anthony looked up at the building. No longer just a room in a building, it was a place—his place. Anthony thought, maybe for the first time since he had been away at school, *I'm home.*

He opened the outer door and held it for two girls coming out. He ducked in behind them and took the stairs two at a time. At the top landing, he turned into the boys' wing. Heading towards his room, he passed Randall's open door, then backed up two steps and walked in—uninvited. Randall was sitting at his desk staring off into space. When Anthony broke into his reverie, he blinked and said, "Hey Anth', have a seat. What's up?"

Anthony walked in and sat on the bed facing Randall. "Not much. What's going on with you?"

"Just trying to figure things out."

"Aren't we all? Anything specific?" Anthony felt like Randall had a pensive mood about him and was trying to get him to open up a bit.

"I am having a problem with Keisha."

"What?" Anthony exclaimed. "You two have the most fun of anyone in this dorm. You are constantly hanging around each other. I see you having deep discussions or laughing hysterically all the time. What could possibly be the problem?"

"You don't understand. The problem is not with her."

"But you just said..."

"There are differences between us." Randall emphasized "differences".

"Yeah! She is a beautiful girl and you're a boy—the perfect differences. I'm still not following."

"In case you haven't noticed, she is black."

"So? This is the 70s. This is California, not the deep South. I think everyone is cool about it. Why? Did someone say something about the both of you?"

"No. Everything is cool up here. But Thanksgiving is coming up. I'd like to bring Keisha home to meet my parents, but..."

"Oh, 'meet the parents' stuff. And you don't think they would..."

"Approve," he said completing the sentence.

"Well, are they Imperial Wizards in the Ku Klux Klan or something?"

"No, but they are 'closet racists.' They would say stuff like, 'We're not better than they are, but we're different than they are,' in a condescending way. They would pass out if I brought her home."

"Hmm. Sort of like, 'Guess Who's Coming to Dinner' all over again."

"Exactly. Heck, I was probably a latent racist, but when I'm with Keisha, I don't see a black person. I see a beautiful person. One I'd like to be with for a long time."

Anthony took a deep breath and let it out slowly, considering all angles of the situation. "What does Keisha think about all of this? Has she said how her parents would feel?"

"No, but could you see me going to Christmas dinner at a black family's house in the inner city? It sounds quite terrifying to me."

"Man, I don't know. That's a tough one. Maybe you won't see her family as black once you get to know them."

"I don't know," Randall concluded while shaking his head.

Anthony thought about sending Randall to see Vance but decided against that. Randall needed more concrete advice. Vance was better for more ethereal things.

"I wish I could help," Anthony said. "But I have no idea how to handle that one. Maybe someday it will be more accepted. In the meantime, you are lucky to have found someone special who thinks the same of you. Not many people find that."

Anthony got up and put a hand on Randall's shoulder consoling him. Then he walked out of the room feeling bad he couldn't do more to help the situation.

CHAPTER 12
Thursday Night

Mary Sue and Anthony decided to be discreet about their relationship. They agreed to meet down in the first-floor lobby so as to not attract too much attention. He arrived from one stairwell, and she came down the other. They quickly slipped out the side door and into the chilly night air. There had been a high-pressure system hanging around the area for a few days now. No rain, but colder air and cloudless days and nights.

Being this far north and in a remote region, the stars at night put on quite a show. As Anthony and Mary Sue walked casually across the campus, people were coming or going to night classes, the library, or any of the many labs at the school.

Anthony pointed up and said. "That's Cassiopeia." They were both impressed with his knowledge. Anthony was glad to see his college education from the first semester was paying off so soon. "And that's Polaris, the North Star."

Mary Sue questioned, "Wouldn't that have to be more to the north?"

Anthony gazed up in one direction. He put one arm up stiffly towards the sky like a surveyor then turned the opposite way like he was trying to get his bearings and gazed again. "Oh, yes. That must be it. They kind of look alike. You know, Polaris is not the brightest object in the night sky. The visible planets look like stars but are much brighter."

"You must have gotten at least a C+ in Astronomy last semester," she teased.

"Well, I missed a few classes."

They sat down on a bench between several trees. The bench had a plaque on it commemorating some old alumni who contributed something to the school. They sat down and surveyed the area. There were beautiful plants and flowers around the trees. The area was sort of dark but the lights from the surrounding buildings cast a subtle light all around it.

"So tell me something about Mary Sue that I don't know," Anthony said breaking the ice.

"Hmmm. I have an older brother who is a high school coach. My parents are apple farmers, which I think I told you already. We have a farm on the east side of Hilland. I almost went to school at our local university but wanted to get away. I am lousy at sports, but I love square dancing."

"People still square dance?" he asked incredulously.

"Don't act like it is silly. It's a big thing in rural parts of the country."

"Do they wear puffy dresses?"

"You mean like Dale Evans? No. I usually wear jeans."

"No, I meant the guys," he teased. She slugged him in the arm.

"Okay, what do you guys do on Saturday night down in BIG Southern California?"

"Well, we don't go to Disneyland. Uh, probably go to a party or something. The party is at the beach or at someone's house—if the parents were away."

She nodded. "And what would you wear to one of those cool parties?"

"A puffy dress of course," he mocked.

She laughed heartily. "No really!"

"Usually jeans, a Hawaiian shirt and flip-flops."

She laughed again. "What kind of jeans?"

"Usually, Levi jeans—501s. Why?"

Raising her eyebrows, "Well, if you wore that to a party in Hilland, you'd get beat up. Seriously."

"And that is why there are no cool parties in Hilland. Why did you ask about the jeans?"

"There are plenty of cool parties in Hilland. And jeans have to be Lee's jeans. Nothing else."

One of the things that Anthony had learned was that it was cool to pretend not to be tough, but to actually be tough. It was a cool comic shtick. Guys who act tough are really kind of a joke—because there is always someone tougher.

"Well, if I ever go to a party in Hilland, I hope you are there to protect me."

She laughed again. They talked about the most trivial of things for over an hour. They laughed and teased and questioned each other back and forth. Finally, the lights in the surrounding buildings went out as it was getting late. The bench area was cast into darkness. She leaned into him and he put his arm around her. In the darkness, he held her and they tenderly kissed.

Back up at the dorms, they ascended the stairs and on the third-floor landing, she turned right and he turned left. She said, "Good night, Antonio."

"Good night, Chablis Girl," he replied. Keisha walked out of the boys' hallway just then; apparently, she had been visiting Randall. She looked sideways at Anthony, then sideways at Mary Sue. She shook her head and walked into the girls' hallway. Mary Sue made big eyes at Anthony, giggled, and then followed Keisha down the hallway.

———————

The occasional evening walks on campus continued once or twice a week. Most conversations were exploratory or theoretical in nature. Exploratory in that they questioned each other about their backgrounds, their experiences, their frustrations, and their fears. It was theoretical in that they discussed the general condition of humanity, the challenges of relationships, or the concept of religion.

Anthony found he enjoyed the intellectual give and take almost as much as he enjoyed being alone with a beautiful girl. They frequented the same bench between the trees on campus. It became "their bench."

Each of the walks culminated in some tender kissing which can only go so far when one is sitting on a public bench on campus with people occasionally walking through the area.

Each of the walks ended back at the dorm, on the third-floor landing, where she would turn right and he would turn left.

"Good night, Antonio."

"Good night, Chablis Girl."

———————

After a month or so, they decided to start dating again, but would continue to be discreet about it. Places to go were somewhat limited in the area. They decided not to go anyplace on campus where they might bump into others from the dorm. One day they decided to drive to the beach. Because Anthony had taken the Greyhound Bus up to school, he did not have a car. Mary Sue did have a car at school however, an old Datsun sport coupe.

They walked down to the parking lot together. Mary Sue jumped in and reached across to unlock the passenger door. Anthony opened it and slid into the seat. They drove across the bridge over Highway 101 and through the residential section of town with its old Victorian homes, little bungalow cottages and a few apartment complexes. Soon they were on a country road, driving through pastures towards the sand dunes in the distance. Although the pastures were bathed in the cold sunshine of November, the sand dunes were shrouded in a grey fog that hugged closely to the coastline.

They drove to the base of the sand dunes and parked the car. They both wore jackets to protect them from the fog and mist. Together they walked up a little trail, then over the dunes towards the beach. As they crested the dunes, Anthony looked around and breathed in the salt air as he surveyed the panorama.

No beach in Southern California looked like this. In SoCal, the beaches were crowded strands of sand with pay-parking lots, chain link fences, and fast-food places just across a busy street behind the fences.

As Anthony looked up and down the coastline, he saw only two people walking together on the beach to the north, and one person sitting on a rock to the south. Somehow, as those people reflected on the issues confronting their souls in this harsh and beautiful environment, it seemed there was just enough distance and privacy between the three groups of beach goers. The entire beach had scattered driftwood from the winter storms that ripped through the many forests that grew along the coast. Not far from where they were standing, the grey smoke from a small campfire, probably lit last night from collected wood on the beach, rose into the breeze and blended into the watercolor grey coastal mist. The same breeze bent the beach grass growing out of the dunes here and there.

Anthony turned around and looked inland. Just beyond the dunes, a group of cows munched lazily on grass along a fence that divided the pasture from the sand. He turned his collar up against the cold, damp wind. Mary Sue grabbed his hand and they walked to the top of a tall sand dune with a commanding view of the surf. They sat down for a while in silence, just listening to the constant low roar of the crashing waves.

"This place is beautiful," Anthony said, stating the obvious.

"I know. I come here sometimes to think," she replied.

"What do you think about?" he questioned.

"Growing up. Life. The future. Where we'll be in thirty or forty years from now. It can be overwhelming at times. I have friends who got married right out of high school. When we talk, they tell me about the new sofa they just bought. The new sofa...I just can't relate to that. I have no interest in that. I am not ready for that. Jim is ready for it, and maybe because he is a little older, that's good. And he wants me to be a part of that life. I'm not ready to order my sofa just yet."

"Well, I am glad you're not. Maybe I could interest you in a little love seat in the meantime!" he quipped.

She laughed and gently punched him in the arm. Their relationship had become more genuine, and they could share the truth about where they were in life and what they were facing.

"What should I do?" she asked. "Sometimes I feel like I can't breathe—like I am suffocating."

"Time," is all he said.

"Time? What do you mean?" she asked further.

"Time will sort things out. It always does. Time is the ultimate universal organizer. Think of it this way, do you watch much football on TV?" She shrugged indicating she watched a little. "Well, sometimes when the game starts, the underdog jumps out to a surprising lead over the favored opponent. But as the game progresses, the better team wears down the opponent, takes the lead, and wins the game. My dad used to say; 'There is a reason the games last for sixty minutes. Time reveals the better team.' The same is true with life. We don't know what direction to take for our future, but it always works itself out over time and we discover our destiny."

Mary Sue stared at him with a quizzical look on her face. "I am doubly shocked. I just don't know what shocks me more—the fact that you, whom I consider to be somewhat goofy at times, could say something so profound, or the fact that you just used a sport metaphor to explain my life to me. That's amazing."

"Well, Jim has had more time because he is older. He has his farm or will very soon. He has his profession, that of being a farmer. And he knows he wants to marry you. Time has done its organizing for him to this point." Anthony paused a bit, then continued, "You're still in school, learning new things, and meeting new people," he bowed slightly meaning he was one of those people. "You are still waiting on time. For that matter, so am I. I don't know what I want. I have no college degree yet, no profession, no 'farm.' I literally have nothing to offer you, but I do think we are good together. Please let enough time pass to see what happens. Time is all I ask."

Mary Sue was intently listening to Anthony. When he was finished speaking, she nuzzled her face against his neck and started sobbing. Anthony put his arm around her and held her tenderly while they listened to the crashing surf of the restless ocean.

CHAPTER 13
Tale of Three Thanksgivings

The exodus from the dorms started early Wednesday morning, the day before Thanksgiving. If a professor had canceled a class or two, some people left late Tuesday evening. Everyone was anxious to travel home, like lemmings moving in a great migration.

Orange County, California

Don drove Anthony to the Northwest Community Airport late Wednesday afternoon. He pulled into the gravel parking lot and let him off at the terminal. The terminal building was a log structure with one ticket booth inside that was shared by three airlines. Anthony jumped out, grabbed his one bag and thanked Don for the ride before he headed off to check in for his flight. Twenty minutes later, the agent at the ticket booth, announced it was time to board. He walked out of the log building to the forty-two inch tall chain link fence. They were boarding through Gate 2, which was just six feet away from Gate 1. He then walked across the concrete to the rolling stairway and boarded the plane.

Twenty minutes later, Anthony's plane was screaming down the runway, before lifting off and heading west before banking to the left and streaking south toward Orange County.

The fifty-minute flight landed on time and taxied toward the terminal building. They had to wait for an open spot to deplane, as even small regional airports were jammed with people the day before Thanksgiving. Finally, the rolling staircase was put in place, and the cabin door opened. One by one the passengers exited the plane and descended the steps.

Once on the tarmac, Anthony could see his parents, sister and Judy on the observation deck on the second level of the terminal building. They all started waving when they spotted him and he waved back. Inside the building, they met by the escalators and it was hugs and kisses all around. Except there was a slight emptiness that Anthony felt when he kissed Judy. *Was it me or was it her?* he wondered.

In the car on the way home from the airport, everyone wanted to know about school. Anthony told them about his classes; a bit more about the fun they were having up at school, the epic of the Big Game, and nothing about Mary Sue.

The next day, Anthony's family got all dressed up and went to an aunt's house for Thanksgiving dinner. The men watched football on television, and the women worked in the kitchen helping Aunt Cecilia with the turkey and all the trimmings.

After one of the pro games on television was over, the turkey dinner was served. In all, there were six cousins, two aunts and two uncles, and all of Anthony's family around the dining room table with a card table extension under the tablecloth. Of course, there were multiple conversations going on in every direction.

"This bean salad is delicious!"

"The Detroit Lions are horrible."

"Can I have some more mashed potatoes?"

"How do you like college?"

"Who do the Rams play on Sunday?"

"Can I have some dessert?"

It was organized chaos. But it had been a family tradition since Anthony was very young. He remembers it started out with just four cousins, but two more came along about the time that Anthony's sister was born— post-war optimism at its peak.

After the meal was over and the table was cleared, the kids and adults brought out the board games. Anthony thought the general term for those games was fairly accurate, but not spelled correctly. It should have been more like "bored games." Anthony dutifully played along for the sake of the younger cousins, but purposely stretched the rules to agitate his older cousins into heated discussions on how to play the game. Finally, it was time for good-byes.

Later, the family drove home and Anthony excused himself so he could go visit Judy at her house. Judy's family was the home team today, and all her relatives invaded their home for several hours to uphold the family tradition on this November holiday.

When Anthony turned on to her street, he had to park several houses down since there were so many of Judy's relatives' cars in her driveway and in front of her house. He walked up the walkway and through the open door. There must have been fifty people in the house and backyard. They must have had to eat in shifts, Anthony thought to himself. He walked into the kitchen and found Judy helping her mother wash the dishes, silverware, pots, pans, serving bowls and everything else used to serve a group of fifty. Anthony kissed Judy, greeted her mom and picked up a towel and started drying dishes.

"So, how'd it go?" he asked her.

"Good. Mom had two turkeys and has been cooking for three days," she said, not looking up from the sink full of dirty pots and pans; her arms in the grey soapy water up to her elbows. "How was your get together?" she politely asked.

"It was fine. Good to be home." Later, when most of the dishes were clean, but before the fifty desert dishes were distributed mounded with treats and sweets, Anthony and Judy walked out into the front yard. Anthony leaned on one of the relative's cars and Judy stood in front of him. He was holding both of her hands with both of his. Judy still seemed distant or distracted.

"Did you know that Tim and Ginny broke up?" she asked. This was shocking news to Anthony. He had just gotten into town last night and hadn't had a chance to even talk to Tim on the phone.

"You're kidding! What happened?" he asked.

"I dunno," she said looking away. "I guess things change." Anthony nodded.

They chatted a while, but Anthony figured there would be no necking tonight since every relative of Judy's from 4 months old to 94 years old were coming in and out of the house constantly—but maybe not the 94 year-old so much.

The next two nights, Anthony hung out with Judy and some friends. Friday night they went to the mall to do some early Christmas shopping. Saturday night they went to a movie. Everyone had a good time, but Anthony just felt like something was missing. Then he realized what it was—Mary Sue. He felt in some way, Judy was sensing this also—even though he hadn't said a thing to her about Mary Sue.

His parents and sister brought Anthony back to the airport on Sunday evening, but Judy was busy and couldn't come along. The terminal was jammed with literally thousands of people trying to catch flights back to their daily realities. Anthony wove his way through the crowds as he carried his suitcase and ticket. He checked in and 30 minutes later than scheduled, boarded the plane.

Once in the air, the 55-minute flight was smooth and when he landed, Don was waiting for him at the gate. There were literally tens of people in the log terminal waiting for their flights to board—thirty-four to be exact.

As they drove back to campus, Don gave Anthony a recap of his Thanksgiving weekend. Anthony wasn't sure what to make of his Thanksgiving.

Berkley, California

On Wednesday morning, Randall and Keisha loaded an Abercrombie & Fitch suitcase in the small trunk of his red Alpha Romero sports car. They were sharing that piece of luggage since they didn't have much stuff and since they were only going to be staying for the long Thanksgiving weekend. Also, Keisha didn't have any luggage of her own. When she arrived on campus in the fall, all her clothes and things were either in cardboard boxes or paper grocery bags. Randall had been perceptive and gracious enough to offer her space in his suitcase. Plus, it would help send a message to his parents that he and Keisha are a couple, something he was sure they would resist.

They drove down the service road and turned left on the frontage road for a bit before getting on to the onramp for Highway 101, south. His car had the convertible top up to protect them from the cold, damp air as they drove south on their way to Berkley.

For the first hour or so, they talked, laughed and listened to music. After a while, they drove in silence taking in the raw, natural beauty of California's northern coastal region. As they got closer to the bay area, the forests thinned out and the buildings increased their density along the freeway. Soon they hit San Raphael and switched from the 101 to the 580. They drove past San Quentin as they started over the Richmond Bridge. Keisha, although nervous about going over the bridge, marveled at the view. A while later, they were pulling up to Randall's parent's house high up on the hillside in an expensive area of Berkley. From his front yard, one could see the bay and part of two bridges in the bay area. The house itself was an old Victorian, but it had been completely restored and looked brand new.

Randall parked facing uphill on the opposite side of the street from his parent's house. He cranked the steering wheel hard to the left and set the parking brake, then jumped out and grabbed the suitcase from the trunk. Together, Randall and Keisha crossed the street and walked up the walkway to the massive double front door. Randall knocked and rang the bell. His father, Randall senior, opened the door and warmly greeted his son and did an admirable job concealing his surprise when he greeted his son's girlfriend—who was black.

"And you are Keisha," he gushed. "We have heard so much about you."

"But not everything I am guessing," she joked as she could tell he was surprised to see her as much as he tried to conceal it.

"Let me get your mother. I think she is in the study," he said excusing himself.

Keisha turned to Randall and quietly grilled him. "You didn't tell them that I am black?" she whispered to him with clenched teeth while making big eyes.

"Well, not yet," he said hesitantly.

Just then his mother entered the foyer with his father trailing behind.

"Randy, I am so glad to see you. And this must be Keisha. Welcome to our house." She too did an excellent job of disguising her shock at seeing that Keisha was black. They adjourned to the family room towards the back of the house and had some polite small talk. Then Randall's mother explained that there were five bedrooms upstairs and they could use any one or two of them as they wished—very open minded of her.

After some more small talk and questions, Emma, the black cook brought in some hors d'oeuvres from the kitchen for everyone to nibble on. The whole time they were talking and eating, Keisha never once spoke in her black dialect, but rather spoke like a law student from U.C. Berkley right down the road.

With her quick wit and humor, she had Randall senior won over as she was joking and teasing him, much to his delight. Several times, he was doubled over in laughter. His mother however was cool and polite, but nothing more. She asked slightly prying questions, but nothing rude or revealing of how unhappy she was with the situation. Even Emma gave Keisha a sidelong glance of disapproval, but said nothing.

Before dinner, Randall who was carrying the luggage, and Keisha went upstairs to select their room—or rooms.

At the top of the stairs, Randall asked, "How do you want to do this?" meaning the sleeping arrangements.

"I think with the looks I am getting from your mom and Emma, we better have separate rooms."

"Okay, you take the one on the right. I'll be in the one on the left. Kind of like in the dorms." Keisha rolled her eyes and grabbed the suitcase from his hand and walked into the bedroom on the right.

She unpacked her stuff and set her clothes on the chair next to the bed, then put her toiletries in the bathroom adjacent to the bedroom. It was the first time in her life that she had a bathroom all to herself.

She then walked into Randall's room and tossed the half empty suitcase to him. He caught it awkwardly and she walked out. He unpacked his stuff and set the suitcase on the far side of the bed.

An hour later, the two of them were back downstairs and seated at the dinner table with his parents. Emma was serving dinner, a seafood dish with a white sauce and steamed vegetables. Although no one else noticed it, when Emma put a scoop of steamed vegetables on her plate, Keisha was sure she banged the spoon loudly against her dish—as a sort of protest to her being at dinner with the family. Maybe it was true or maybe it was just all in her mind, she thought.

Through the polite dinner conversation, Randall's mom had established that Keisha... lived in south central Los Angeles, and had five siblings, two older, and three younger. The two older siblings, a brother and a sister, were not currently in school and apparently were not working either. She owned no car. She did however get good grades in high school, did well on her SAT tests, and qualified for a combination of scholarships and grants to pay for her college education.

After dinner, Emma served a fruit sorbet with a sliced kiwi on top in a parfait dish. Keisha looked at her parfait dish and to her, it obviously contained the smallest scoop of sorbet and the kiwi looked like it had been butchered instead of sliced. She just forced a grin and ate it.

After dinner, the travelers were tired, so they both headed upstairs for some sleep, each to their own rooms. On the way up the stairs, Keisha whispered to Randall, "I don't know who is going to stab me in my sleep tonight, your mom, the interrogator; or Emma."

"Hey, look on the bright side," he responded, "My dad loves you. I can tell."

"Great! That means I have won over 33 percent of the household."

"Hey, in baseball, a 33 percent batting average is 330 and you're on the All-Star team."

She rolled her eyes again, went into her room and closed the door. She slept with one eye open, looking for anyone carrying a large butcher knife.

Early Thanksgiving morning, Keisha quietly came down the stairs of the spacious house. She could see the light on in the kitchen, probably Emma working on the dinner. She pushed the swinging door open and saw Emma chopping up toasted bread for the turkey stuffing. Emma, somewhat startled to an intrusion so early in the morning, completely ignored Keisha.

"Why don't you like me?" Keisha said coming right to the point.

"I don't think about you one way or the other," Emma said without looking up from her chopping. Keisha noticed the large knife in her hand.

"Well, I think you don't like me and I don't understand why," Keisha added.

"I have worked for this family for twenty years, since before Master Randall was born," Emma said starting to open up a little.

"You call him Master, like a 'slave master'?" Keisha was shocked.

"No, you book-smart girl. Like he is the son in the family. Mister Randall is the father and Master Randall is the son," Emma went on explaining.

"Oh," said Keisha, embarrassed by her ignorance of that tradition.

"Anyway, I have worked for this family for twenty years and they have always treated me good. I love them like they is my own. And I don't want no street-smart woman comin' in here messing things up, be she white or black or brown."

"I am not going to mess anything up," Keisha started. "I met 'Master' Randall at school and we hit it off immediately. I know he is white and I am black. But when I look at him, I don't see that difference. I see someone who treats me nice and sees me for what I am and what I might become. That is a huge gift to me. No one has ever done that for me before. And I think I do the same thing for him. You just said that you have known him for all his life. Well, does he look happy?" Emma nodded grudgingly. "It's like your stuffing. Individually, the breadcrumbs, onions, celery and chicken broth all taste good, but together they taste great. When we are together, I think we are great."

"And don't forget the parsley and sage," Emma said, proud of her recipe.

"You put parsley and sage in your stuffing?" she asked.

"Look-a here child, you chop up one cup of parsley and a quarter cup of sage. Then you mix 'em in with two beaten eggs and you have the best damn turkey stuffin' ever."

A little while later, Randall walked into the kitchen looking for a cup of coffee and was taken back by seeing Keisha and Emma laughing and talking together. In fact, Keisha insisted on helping (under the guise of learning) make the stuffing.

After a long morning of watching parades and football on TV, Randall's older sister, Karen and her husband arrived and were greeted warmly by all. Her husband Gary was carrying a casserole bowl of green bean salad and set it on the Norman Rockwell-style Thanksgiving table.

Soon, the six of them were seated around the table saying the blessing. Emma carried the turkey, then all the side dishes, one after the other, through the swinging door between the kitchen and the dining room and began filling everyone's plate. Keisha noticed that Emma didn't bang the spoon on her plate while serving, which she took as a small victory. Everyone was being polite and enjoying light conversation.

While everyone was enjoying the delicious Thanksgiving dinner, Randall's dad looked up and asked him, "Guess who's coming to dinner...next week?"

Randall looked up incredulously. "DAD!" Keisha almost choked on her cranberry sauce. Both of them thought he was referencing the 1967 movie starring Sidney Poitier, Spencer Tracy and Katharine Hepburn.

"What?" Randall senior said very confused. "Your old friend George, his parents are coming over," he explained. "Your mom and I haven't seen them in several years now. They moved to Palm Springs but are going to be in town next week." He still didn't understand the reason for his son's brief outburst.

Young Randall gathered his composure, and said, "Well, give them my best and tell them to say, 'Hi' to George." Keisha and Randall looked at each other stifled a laugh at their misunderstanding.

Friday and Saturday, Randall showed Keisha some of the sights in the East Bay area, among them, the campus of the University of California at Berkley, and Jack London Square. Keisha enjoyed them all, but was most enthralled with the view of the bay and the Golden Gate Bridge in the distance.

After dinner on Saturday, Emma was cleaning up in the kitchen. Keisha was in the family room watching television with Randall senior. They were conversing and laughing out loud and having a great time.

Randall walked out on the small back patio deck and saw his mother sitting in a lounge chair. "What are you thinking about Mom?" he asked, unaware of the torrent he was about to unleash.

"Randy, I just don't like her. Keisha just seems so loud and opinionated. She always seems so confrontational. And I worry about her background."

"Mom, that's just the way she is. She is a living example of the 'American Dream' that you and Dad keep talking about. She is the first person in her family to ever go to college. She had none of the benefits that I had growing up. No encyclopedia sets, no books to read, no trips to the museums, or to art galleries, or anything. She had loving parents who just happened to be poor. They nurtured and loved her like you and Dad did for me, but she had none of the things to help her elevate her station in life. She <u>had</u> to be assertive and ask questions and challenge both her teachers and her classmates. If she would have politely sat in the back of the class and never said anything, she would become just like her parents, poor and without an education," he paused for a moment before continuing.

"Because she did pester her teachers for explanations, and asked them to repeat it or rephrase it, she has gone farther in school than anyone in her family. She had to do that, because unlike me, there was no one at home to help explain stuff. Her parents loved her, but they didn't have the education to explain algebra or physics to her like you and Dad were able to do for me. For her to be successful, she had to assert herself, and she did. That's why she will one day graduate, and get a good job and lift herself out of the poverty in which she was raised. I respect her, and admire her for that."

"You make it sound like we are racist. It has nothing to do with her being black," she said emphatically.

"Mom, I think it has EVERYTHING to do with her being black. It is just too much for you and Dad to accept. She is not the white, Anglo-Saxon, protestant, blonde, baby-making machine that you pictured me with," Randall argued.

"Your Father and I are NOT racist," she said getting more agitated.

"You do realize that the only people who say, 'I am not racist', are racists," Randall pointed out.

"Your Father and I have black friends. Not a lot of them, but we do."

"So, your black friends, the few of them you do have, proves that you aren't racist—but you don't want your son to marry one of them," he shot back.

"YOU'RE GOING TO MARRY HER NOW?" his mom said practically screaming.

Randall continued, "What would your friend, Barbara Johnson say if her son David could walk into her house once again and he brought a black girlfriend, or for that matter, a gay boyfriend home with him—and said they were going to get married? What would she say, Mom?" he implored.

His mom gasped in shock. What Randall had said was the equivalent of a verbal punch in the face. His mom's best friend was Barbara Johnson. Her son David, who was five years older than Randall had been drafted into the army and sent to Vietnam. After being in country for several months, he was on leave in Saigon with several buddies from his unit. While having a beer at what looked like an old French café, he wanted to get his boots shined. A shoeshine boy approached and set his box down in front of David but had to go retrieve his brush. While waiting for him to return, David put his boot on the foot-space on top of the shoeshine box where the boy did his work. When he did this, the weight of his foot on the foot-space detonated a powerful bomb in the shoeshine box, instantly killing David, all his buddies, and most everyone in and around the café. The blast was so powerful, there wasn't even a body left to ship home to his mother—no son for her to bury.

It was a horrible, gut-wrenching experience that had brought the horrors of war from the evening news on the TV set, right into Randall's mother's life.

"I'll tell you what she would do; Mrs. Johnson would hug her son <u>and</u> whoever he brought home with him, no matter what," Randall concluded.

His mom was speechless. She put a hand over her mouth to stifle a cry and got up from the lounge chair and ran inside the house.

Early Sunday morning, Randall and Keisha prepared to go back to school. Randall loaded the suitcase in the trunk. Randall senior shook his son's hand and gave Keisha a big warm hug. Emma gave them both a little bag of homemade cookies for a treat on the road. Randall's mom politely said good-bye to both of them in an icy sort of way. As they drove off, Randall gave a huge sigh of relief. He realized it was not as good as he had hoped, but not as bad as it could have been.

All the way back up to school, Keisha and Randall, laughed, talked and enjoyed the scenery; but they both felt a bit subdued as they reflected on their differences and the challenges their relationship would bring them.

Hilland, Washington

The Datsun sport coupe started on the third turn of the key in the ignition and Mary Sue drove down the service road towards the onramp to Highway 101, north. She drove along the scenic highway without really noticing the natural beauty all around her. Her mind was focused on her 12-hour drive and what was waiting for her at home.

The last few weeks, she had enjoyed Anthony's companionship, humor and tenderness; all without feeling any level of commitment toward a serious relationship with him. She felt like she could breathe when she was with him. It wasn't a Bohemian lifestyle, but it was more in line with what a girl, one year out of high school, should be experiencing at this age. They were not picking out china patterns or sofa fabric. They were collecting driftwood on the beach; they went on quiet walks across campus or through the woods; they were going to the movies. And most importantly, they were having deep conversations and spirited debates, as they were two intelligent people who were getting to know each other—all without commitment, judgment, or ownership.

Mary Sue turned off Highway 101 in Crescent City and on to the 199, then over to Interstate 5 in Grants Pass. She continued north on Interstate 5 through Portland, where she had lunch, and then on to Tacoma where she switched to the 18, then the 90, 970, 97, and then the 2 into Hilland.

Getting off the highway, she drove through her hometown; past the grade school she attended, past the church where she was a member, past the bakery where she had worked a few summers ago. She seemed to be more aware of the chipped paint and rusted pipes on the buildings, and trash in the alleyways as she drove through the small sun-faded and worn business district of Hilland. She was torn between the feeling of nostalgia of being someplace where she was totally familiar and comfortable; and the feeling of suffocating because it was all too familiar and too comfortable. As she drove, the words to Simon and Garfunkel's new song, "My Little Town," echoed in her head. Did she really want to be born, grow up, and die in the same place? Her feelings were very conflicted.

As the sun was beginning to set, she concluded the long drive and turned off the main road out of town, and down a gravel road. From there, she turned through a chain link fence into the front yard of her parents' house and farm. The apple trees in the orchard, now bare of all leaves, stood like silent sentinels on three sides of the castle that had always been Mary Sue's home.

She drove near the house, parked behind a Ford F-150 pick-up truck and pulled the lever ratcheting on the parking brake. The pick-up truck told her that Jim was here visiting her family. In fact, there he was, sitting on one of the rockers on the front porch with her dad. She got out of the Datsun and stretched her back, aching from the long ride.

"There's my girl!" Jim exclaimed as he rose from the chair.

Ownership, Mary Sue thought to herself, focusing on the word, "my."

"How was the trip?" he asked.

"Good. Long," she replied.

Jim came bounding down the three stairs to the porch and jogged over to her, while she was still stretching her aching back. He scooped her up in his arms and kissed her warmly and passionately. Taking her hand and grabbing her luggage, he led her up the porch where she bent over and kissed her father lovingly on the forehead. He looked older and more tired than she had remembered him when she had left for school—much like the town of Hilland itself.

"Where's Mama?"

"Oh, she's inside Sweet Pea. She'll be so glad that you are home. Neither of us like you driving that long road all by yourself." "Sweet Pea" was his pet name for his daughter. Mary Sue let go of Jim's hand and opened the screen door to the house. She went around the staircase and down the hallway to the kitchen in back of the house. Her mom was working at the counter when she looked up and saw Mary Sue.

"There she is! How are you, Honey?" Mama exclaimed as she tightly hugged her daughter. Mary Sue got choked up, as she became keenly aware of the passing of time, as she had never been aware of before.

"I'm fine Mama," she said as she wiped a tear from her eye before anyone could notice. "I just need a drink of water."

That evening, her family along with Jim had dinner together. Afterwards, they sat in the living room talking and watching television. Her father sat in a well-worn recliner. Her mom sat in a rocking chair opposite her father. Jim had his arm around Mary Sue as they sat together on the sofa. She was tired and wasn't really listening to the conversation or what was on television.

"So, did you hear what Jim said, Mary?" her mom asked.

"Uh, no. I wasn't really listening," she replied.

"I said that I think this is going to be a very special Christmas for us," Jim repeated as he looked for her reaction.

"I am sure it will be," she smiled; pretty sure she knew what he was hinting. "I'm pretty tired, I think I'm going to go to bed now. I'll see you tomorrow, dear." She kissed him and said goodnight to her parents.

Upstairs in her room, she looked at her school photos that were framed and hanging on the wall; her many 4-H ribbons hanging about her window; and the collection of childhood memorabilia from her grade school and high school years.

She unbuttoned her blouse and tossed it casually on the chair across from her bed. Next, she reached down and unbuckled her western belt and stepped out of her Lee's jeans. She reached behind her back and undid her lacy bra and placed it on top of her blouse. She looked at her clothes on the chair and thought that they looked as tired as she felt.

When she went to the dresser to get her nightgown, she passed her oak-framed wardrobe mirror. She stopped and stepped back so she could view her own, nearly nude reflection.

As she stood in front of her mirror observing that her body was beginning to be more curvaceous, she pondered that her life had moved beyond the things of childhood and 4-H project and high school dances. Her body told her that adulthood and all that came with it was just ahead.

She put her right hand on her opposite shoulder. Her arm crossed over her bare breasts as if she were trying to hide them from herself in the mirror, thus denying the passage of time and allowing her to believe she was still childlike.

Then her arm slid back down to her side and she realized that her maturing body was desirable and that in turn, stirred a womanly warmth in her.

The next day, Mary Sue helped her mom in the kitchen as she prepared a huge turkey dinner and all the fixings for their family, several relatives that lived nearby, and Jim. By late morning, most of the guests had arrived.

Jim was a "roll-up his sleeves" kind of guy and Mary Sue always appreciated that about him. He helped Mary's father set up the long folding tables that reached from the dining area to halfway across the living room, and then he set up all the folding chairs for the guests who were getting hungrier by the minute.

After snacking on chips and dip, a raw vegetable platter, and cheese bread, any hint of hunger would be completely obliterated by the main course that Mary's mom proudly carried to the table. Her father started to carve the turkey, but was struggling, so he asked Jim to take over for him.

To Mary Sue, this was another reminder of how Jim was so accepted in their family. But he had earned that acceptance by always being there for her, and for her parents. Still, their marriage was a foregone conclusion, the wedding, just a rubber-stamp of the inevitable. She again had the feeling that she could not breathe. She excused herself from the table just after the blessing was said and walked through the kitchen and out the back door. She took a deep breath and wandered past the barn and into the apple orchard. The trees' lifeless-looking branches were reaching up like skeletal arms trying to warn her about the future. She started to hyperventilate.

"Sis? Are you alright?" It was her older brother Bob who had followed her outside to check on her.

Somewhat startled, she gasped a deep breath of air, "I am fine. I'm fine. It is so good to see you. I'm glad you and Cindy could come down for the day."

"Ah, we wouldn't miss it. It is always good to be home. So, are you and Jim making any announcements any time soon?"

"Not that I am aware of," she said turning away to hide her anxiety.

"How about you two? You've been married going on two years. When do you think you'll start a family?" she said desperately trying to change the subject.

"We think maybe this year or next we will start a family." They talked a bit more as they headed back to the house. Inside they took their places at the extended table, Bob next to Cindy and Mary Sue next to Jim.

That evening, as Mary Sue lay in bed trying to go to sleep, her mind drifted to Anthony; and the person she is, and the freedom she feels when she is up at school. It was not only a different place; it was a place where she was a different person.

On Friday, Mary Sue helped her mom clean up after the feast from the day before. She also did some cleaning upstairs in the bedrooms and bathrooms—things that her mother didn't seem to notice or hadn't had the energy to complete.

The next day, Mary Sue drove her Datsun over to Jim's family farm. After lunch, some mutual friends from their high school days stopped by to visit. They sat around in the family room talking and watching some college football on television. The guys were analyzing why one team was having so much difficulty scoring; while the girls were talking about the new dining room set one of them had recently purchased and what a great deal they had gotten on it. Mary Sue's eyes glazed over. She wanted to be sitting on a sand dune, looking out over the ocean and thinking about the many possibilities of her future; not sitting here facing the certainty of her predictable future.

Early Sunday morning, her folks were on the porch as Jim loaded her suitcase in the back of the Datsun. Mary Sue waved to her parents one last time and then turned and hugged Jim. He was warm, strong, caring and gave her everything she needed. She realized that she was indeed fortunate. They kissed warmly and then she started the car on the third turn of the key in the ignition.

"I can fix that," Jim said. *Of course, he could,* thought Mary Sue as she drove down the dirt road, through town and back on the highway, heading back to school.

CHAPTER 14
Getting Warmer

Once back on campus, Anthony stopped by to
visit Mary Sue. She seemed happy and excited to see
him. They both told each other what they had done
over the long weekend, leaving out any mention of Jim
or Judy.

Anthony asked if she wanted to go on a walk that
night. Mary Sue said that she wanted to go, but she was
tired.

"Can we go another night this week?" she asked.

"Sure," he said. He leaned into her and kissed
her as she kissed him back.

Returning to his hallway, Anthony noticed
Randall's door open, so he stopped by to see how things
had gone for him over the long weekend.

"Well?" Anthony said as he walked in to the
room.

Randall gave a big exhale and looked back at
Anthony with a smirk.

"I guess slightly better than I had expected. No,
I'll say it was definitely better than I expected," he said
correcting himself. "Dad took it much better than Mom
did. I think he really ended up liking Keisha. They
laughed and talked and seemed to get along just great.
My mom on the other hand, just about had a meltdown
over it. She was not pleased, and the worst part was,
she wouldn't admit that race was the issue—when it
was obvious that it was the issue. The real interesting
part that I hadn't even considered was how Emma, our
cook would react to her. At first, she was not happy—
and I think it was because Keisha is black! Here Emma
is black, and she's shooting daggers at Keisha from

across the room. It was crazy. As Emma got to know her though, I think it turned out fine. Crazy weekend though. And wait till I tell you what Dad said at dinner..." Randall went on and told Anthony about his dad's comment about, "Guess who's coming to dinner?" and they both howled in laughter.

"Well, I guess you survived and that's the important thing. And your mom will come around eventually," Anthony said reassuringly. Randall thanked him for his support and returned to his studying. Anthony walked out the door and up the hallway to his room.

After the drive to the beach the week before Thanksgiving, Anthony and Mary Sue wanted to continue to date regularly once they were again back at school. Occasionally they would go to the beach, although Anthony figured Mary Sue might sometimes go there by herself. Other times they'd go to the movies in town. And they still enjoyed their evening walks across the campus.

Later that first week back at school, they went on a late evening walk around the campus. After the usual sitting on the bench by the trees kissing, they were still a bit flushed from their passion as they walked back to the dorm. They walked up the stairs hand-in-hand and as usual, he turned left...but she wouldn't let go of his hand and also turned left, walking with him down the quiet hall.

Don was still studying in the library. The other hallway doors, a few usually open, somehow, were now all quiet and shut. Anthony sensed that the sympathetic hallway had purposely closed its eyes so it would not be a witness to their complicated and secretive romance.

Walking to his room, he opened the door for Mary Sue and followed her inside.

She went over and sat on his bed while he grabbed a shoe from his closet. He pulled both ends of the shoelace to give him a lot of slack to work with, and then tied both ends together near the aglet. Opening the door slightly, he hung the shoe on the doorknob by the shoelace and gently closed the door locking it with a soft, nearly silent but almost guilty click. He hoped Don would get the message.

Closing the door, Anthony turned off the bright ceiling light, so the only light in the room were from the lights outside on campus which filtered through their window. He turned towards Mary Sue and slid next to her as she sat on the bed. Putting his arm around her, he kissed her passionately. As she lay back, both of them swung their legs up on to the bed and the rest of the world fell away.

Don trudged up the stairs a little after 11 p.m. when the library closed. He was carrying several textbooks and a notebook of his work. At the top of the stairs, he turned left and headed down the hallway toward his room. Bleary-eyed from studying it wasn't until he was standing in front of the door and reaching for the key in his pocket that he saw the shoe hanging from the door. He paused a minute while he pondered what this meant.

As he lay in the darkness of the room, Anthony could see light from the hallway coming underneath the door. At a little after 11 p.m. Anthony saw two feet walk up to his door and stop. He knew it was Don and hoped he figured out what the shoe on the door meant. He was ready to call out if Don put his key in the lock. The two feet stood there for a few long seconds, then walked away. Anthony turned and pulled the covers up a little higher over both of them.

Don walked down to the restrooms, set his books on the bench and proceeded wash up and brushed his teeth; all the things he normally does before heading to bed. When he was finished, he grabbed his books and walked back up the hallway, past his room and the shoe and walked into the little study lounge. There was a soft cushioned chair next to a table and a lamp. He set his books on the table and moved another chair, so it faced the chair by the lamp. He sat down, put his feet up on the second chair, turned on the light and started reading another chapter from his textbook until he fell asleep around midnight.

At around 2 a.m., Anthony awoke to find himself alone in his bed. He looked around and Don's bed was empty too. Turning on the light, he saw that his shoe was on the floor just inside the door. He quickly threw on some clothes and opened the door and looked up and down the empty hallway. Maybe Don went to someone else's room for the night. Then he thought, no, Don wouldn't do that because then he would have to explain why he couldn't be in his own room. Don wouldn't do that to Anthony or Mary Sue. He understood the secretiveness of the relationship.

Anthony walked down the hall and looked around the restroom—no one. He then walked up the hallway and saw the light on in the little study lounge. There was Don, slumped over in the chair, with his book on his lap, sound asleep. Anthony gently nudged his shoulder waking him and said, "All clear. You can come in now."

Don, still groggy from sleeping in an awkward position, looked around to get his bearings. Then he stood up, picked up his books, and followed Anthony back to their room.

Once inside, they turned out the lights and both of them got in their beds. In the darkness, Don said, "Omertá."

Anthony clarified, "There is no Omertá to Omertá about."

"That's what I mean, I won't say anything to anyone," Don replied.

"But there's nothing to say, if you know what I mean," Anthony tried to explain.

"I know exactly what you mean. Your secret is safe with me."

"No Don, there is nothing to say; there is no secret, there is no Omertá."

"Then why was there a shoe hanging on the doorknob?" he asked.

"Go to sleep Don," Anthony said, exhausted from trying to explain.

"You'll have to tell it all to me in the morning, Bro," said Don just before they both fell asleep.

An hour earlier at around 1 a.m., Mary Sue had kissed Anthony as he slept. Quietly, she got out of bed and adjusted her clothes and hair. She opened the door slightly and peeked up and down the hallway. Grabbing the shoelaces, she removed the shoe from the doorknob and tossed it back into the darkness of the room. Stepping out into the hallway, she quietly closed the door behind her. As she walked back towards her room, she was still a little breathless over what they had done and thankful for what they had not done.

CHAPTER 15
Winter Wonderland

December 1974

At the beginning of December, the excitement was growing in the dorms in anticipation of Christmas. Some, who were filled with the holiday spirit, did some decorating of their dorm room doors for the holidays, although everyone knew that the dorms would be completely empty by Friday evening, December 20th and would remain that way until Saturday, January 4th, the first day that students could return to the dorms.

Mixed in to this punch bowl of holiday cheer was the stress of knowing final exams were just two weeks away. Some students who had been putting off completing projects and big assignments in favor of partying all night long for the last several months were now working overtime to improve their grades. They had been eating dessert all semester, but now they had to eat some vegetables.

Anthony and Mary Sue were now an "item" although still being careful not to let others know about their relationship. When they were off campus, they were enjoying their time together going to movies, bookstores, and restaurants. Both knew that Christmas break was just around the corner and that it would pull them apart...in so many different ways. But for right now, the weather was crisp, and there was nothing like being in love during the holidays.

On their evening walks, they had to bundle up because the temperature was dropping into the high thirties when the sun went down. When they would talk, they could see their steamy breath in the cold air. They still sat on "their" bench near the trees but did not stay there very long because of the cold. Eventually, they would return to Anthony's dorm room and "warm-up" together. Don did a lot of studying in the library on those evenings.

Anthony wanted to give Mary Sue a Christmas present before they left for the holidays, but he had no idea what to get her. Mary Sue was facing the same dilemma. Money was always an issue for college students, so the challenge was to find a gift that was both meaningful and practically free.

With just two days before Christmas break, Anthony was getting more on edge about Mary Sue returning home... to Jim... at Christmas... under the mistletoe. He also wanted to give her his Christmas present just before she left for Christmas break. They decided to exchange gifts at their bench in the trees when they went on their walk that evening.

After dinner in the dining hall, Anthony hurried back to his dorm room. He put on his heavy coat and grabbed his gift for Mary Sue. Carrying it like a football under his arm, he walked into the girls' hallway towards Mary's room. Her door was open and she was just putting on her heavy jacket as he walked through the door. She picked up a small box and put it in her pocket. They walked together down the hallway, down the stairs and took their usual path across campus to the bench between the trees. They were both cold and shivering a bit even though they were wearing heavy coats. They sat next to each other on the bench and talked casually about the excitement of going home and how much they would miss each other over the break.

"Well, do you want to exchange gifts now," Anthony asked, anxious to give his gift to her.

"Yes," she said excitedly.

Anthony handed his gift to Mary Sue. It was a shoebox with a 3x5 card taped to the lid. On the 3x5 card was a primitive, red felt pen drawing of a Christmas bow.

"I hope you didn't pay extra for gift wrapping," she said jokingly.

"Hey, I took valuable time away from my studies to draw that bow," he said playing along in mock indignation.

"I love how you wrapped it," she assured him. Opening it carefully, there was something wrapped in the tissue paper that had been wrapped around the shoes, which had previously occupied the box. Carefully, she took it out and folded back the tissue paper. It was a driftwood and seashell mobile. As she lifted the larger piece, the seashells started swaying as they hung from the various smaller branches of driftwood.

"You made this?" she asked in wonder. "I love it!"

"Well, it was a group effort to be honest. Don drove me back down to the beach where we were. We collected the driftwood and shells. Then, I borrowed some light fishing line from Hector. Don drilled the holes in the shells and driftwood in the Engineering Lab. It helps to know people in high places. And I assembled it with Don helping me find the balancing points," he explained.

Mary Sue held it up and watched it slowly pirouette in front of her.

"I wanted you to always have a little part of the beach we visited together. You can hang it in your room. It is our special place."

Wiping a tear from her eye, she set the mobile back in the box. Then Mary Sue handed her gift to

Anthony. It was a small, gift-wrapped box. Anthony smiled and removed the red ribbon from the box. Taking off the wrapping paper, he opened the box and looked inside. He reached in and took out an old wristwatch with a well-worn watchband. He was curious and looked at her for an explanation.

"When we were on the beach, you said that time would sort things out. You said that all you asked of me was for time. This is my gift to you. I am trying to give you that time. This symbolizes that time," she concluded.

"I don't know what to say. Where did you get it?" he asked, now wiping tears from his eyes. Don would be so pissed.

"I bought it from the thrift store in town. I don't even think it works."

"Its perfect. Thank you. It is a treasure," he said before leaning forward and kissing her most tenderly.

They walked back to the dorm and slowly climbed the stairs. Don was in the room packing his stuff for Christmas Break, so Anthony and Mary Sue kissed at the top of the stairs and said good-bye. He turned to the left, and she turned to the right. They started to walk in different directions, each with their arm extended and their fingers still intertwined, keeping them together for a few seconds longer.

"Merry Christmas Antonio."

"Merry Christmas, Chablis Girl."

And they let go of each other.

———————

After that, chaos reigned. That night, and Friday morning, students all over campus were packing clothes and stuffing gifts in suitcases. They were running down the stairs and jumping in cars, going to the airport or the bus station—all at the pace of people evacuating before a hurricane or abandoning a sinking ship.

Third floor was part of the evacuation. Randall and Keisha had left Thursday night heading toward Los Angeles to spend the holidays with her family. Mary Sue had left early Friday morning driving to Hilland.

Don and Anthony were also ready to abandon ship. Anthony had his things packed and his plane ticket for a noon flight on Friday into Orange County. Don had his stuff packed and was going to drop off Anthony at the airport before driving back to his home near Santa Maria. It was going to be an early drop-off as Don was anxious to get on the road. Anthony was fine with that and was prepared to hang around the terminal for a few hours waiting for his flight.

At 8 a.m., the two of them grabbed their stuff, locked the door to their room and were one of the last ones to leave the dorm for the holidays. There was an eerie silence in the hallway, as well as out on campus. It was like a scene from a sci-fi movie where the city is abandoned because the UFO's were landing. The only sound on campus was the flagpole chain clanging against the steel flagpole.

Anthony sat in the Terminal waiting for his flight when one of the three ticket agents who shared the one ticket booth announced that the Orange County flight had been delayed by thirty minutes. No problem, he thought; more time for him to relax. He went to the vending machine in the corner, bought a candy bar and settled back to watch the twenty-five people or so coming and going through the terminal. Obviously, it was a busy day with Christmas right around the corner.

Finally, his flight was ready to board. He carried his suitcase and ticket to Gate 1, which was six feet away from Gate 2, walked across the concrete and climbed the rolling stairs and boarded his plane. Fifteen minutes later, the jet roared down the runway and climbed westward, before banking to the left and turning southward toward Orange County.

Fifty minutes later, the tires on the landing gear smoked as they touched down on the runway in Orange County. As he walked down the stairway from the plane, he felt the warm, Southern California sun on his face. Looking up, he saw his dad on the observation deck. Walking inside the airport, he met up with his father and they jumped in the car and headed for home.

His dad explained that his mother was busy at home baking for the Christmas Eve dinner, which would be held at their house this year—they were going to be the home team. His sister was Christmas shopping with friends. And Judy was wrapping presents for her mom. Anthony was quiet as they drove the rest of the way home.

They arrived at Anthony's house about mid-afternoon. His mom hugged him even though she had flour on her hands and arms from baking Christmas cookies. He put his suitcase in his bedroom and made some lunch as his mother continued baking. They talked casually about the upcoming invasion of relatives, last-minute Christmas shopping, and all the traffic at the shopping mall.

After lunch, Anthony drove over to Judy's house. She was in her room, still wrapping gifts. There were wrapping paper pieces all over the floor. She was surprised when he walked in her room. He greeted her and kissed her on the forehead as she sat on the floor among gifts, scotch tape, and rolls of wrapping paper.

After the usual questions about his flight, and plans for Christmas Day, Anthony changed the subject.

"Judy, I was thinking, maybe with me at school and you down here at home, like maybe we should take some time apart," he said trying to put it as delicately as he could.

"You mean like you want to break-up?" she questioned.

"Its not that I don't care for you. You know that I do. I just think with it being your senior year of high school, and me not being here, I just don't think it is fair to you," as if he were only thinking of her best interests. He waited for the explosion of anger and a waterfall of tears.

"Well, I was kind of thinking the same thing. In fact, I kind of wanted to ask Tim to take me to the Valentine's Dance coming up since you are up at school."

"Yeah uh...WHAT?" he said quite surprised. "You're going to go to the dance, WITH MY BEST FRIEND?" He couldn't believe it.

"Don't raise your voice to me!" she shouted back. You knew that Tim and Ginny broke up a while ago. You know we have always been close. And, after all, you came over here to break up with me! It shouldn't matter to you WHO I go out with now!"

He could see her logic, but it still didn't seem right. And he was going to have a long talk to Tim about this at some point, although she did say that "she" was going to ask Tim out. She didn't say that Tim had asked her out.

They were silent for a bit, him sitting on the edge of her bed, and her still sitting on the floor. Finally, she reached up and grabbed a box, which said clock radio on the side, from a pile of unwrapped gifts and threw it at him.

"Here, Merry Christmas. That's one less gift I'll have to wrap," she said disgustingly.

Catching the gift awkwardly he said, "I'll bring my gift over after I go to the mall tomorrow."

"Don't bother!" she yelled in reply.

Anthony took that as his queue to leave, so he stood up with the clock radio and headed toward the front door. Judy's mom, who was baking in the kitchen saw Anthony and yelled, "Have a Merry Christmas!" not knowing what had just transpired.

"You too," he yelled back. He set the clock radio on a little table in the entryway and walked out the door. He jumped in his car and drove home. *Merry Christmas indeed,* he said to himself.

The rest of the Christmas holiday went very fast with relatives and friends coming and going. Anthony never did talk to Tim as he went out of state with his family for Christmas. He did go the mall and bought a nice sweater for Judy. He had it gift-wrapped and signed the little card. One evening after Christmas, he drove over to Judy's house and quietly left the gift on her front porch. Two days later, the gift-wrapped box was back on Anthony's front porch and looked like it had been stomped and kicked like a soccer ball. It was a good thing he kept the receipt for the sweater.

New Years Eve was relatively calm. He went to a party with some friends from high school. At twelve midnight when everyone cheered and hugged and kissed, he politely kissed the younger sister of one of his friends who was also at the party. She was a junior in high school and very cute, but there were no sparks between them. He came home at about 12:30 a.m.—out just long enough to say he celebrated.

On New Year's Day, Anthony gorged himself on college football bowl games and all the snacks that his mother set out for the family to enjoy. Thursday and Friday were rather anti-climactic—especially when Anthony had to stand in line at the mall returning the sweater.

Anthony wondered how Mary Sue was doing in Hilland. He felt good about having broken things off with Judy, even though it was a bit difficult, and he was looking forward to Saturday when he would fly back to school.

CHAPTER 16
Adios Antonio

January 1975

After the weeklong celebration from Christmas through New Year's, there is naturally a bit of an emotional letdown. Add to that the thought of leaving home again and heading back to school, and it can be downright depressing. Still, Anthony was excited to return to Sequoia State so he could see Mary Sue again. Because of the short duration of their winter break, they hadn't written any letters to each other. Anthony was a bit apprehensive about how Mary Sue's relationship with Jim would play out during the holidays. A certain jealousy churned beneath the surface.

On Saturday January 4, Anthony boarded a flight from Orange County to the Northwest Community Airport near the university. On the flight up the coast, Anthony watched from his window seat as the terrain below changed from golden, dry brush in the south, to a rich deep green in the north. It really was a different world. The last 15 minutes of the flight, the view of the ground became enshrouded in a solid grey cloud cover. Descending through it, the plane soon bounced on the runway and decelerated quickly. Making a sharp turn at the end of the runway, the plane taxied to the gates. There were only two gates—Gate 1 and Gate 2 were only six feet apart. They would be using Gate 2—as if it mattered. As Anthony descended the roll-up stairway from the jet, he saw Don, leaning on the fence waiting for him.

As Don drove Anthony back to the campus, they talked about what they did over the break and what presents they received for Christmas. Then Anthony asked if very many people were back in the dorms yet.

Don said that only a few had returned, but figured in the next day or so, they would all be returning as classes started on the following Wednesday. Don knew that Anthony was indirectly asking about Mary Sue. She hadn't returned yet as far as Don knew.

Anthony unpacked his stuff, restocked his desk with school supplies and relaxed the rest of the day. As he puttered around his room, he went to his bookshelf on the wall and took down Judy's photo. He wasn't sure what to do with it, so he put it in the cabinet above his closet with his empty luggage. On Sunday, he and Don slept in a bit, but soon got up, as the noise from people moving back into the dorms grew louder. They dressed quickly and headed down the path to the dining hall. There, Buzz greeted them and made delicious California omelets for both of them.

Feeling full after eating, the pair slowly headed back up the path toward the dorms. As they were walking, they saw Shelley coming the other way. As they got closer, Anthony nodded and was about to ask if Mary Sue was back yet. Before he could speak, Shelley burst out with the big news, "Did you hear? Mary Sue got engaged on Christmas Eve. Isn't that great!" Shelley was one of the few who knew about Anthony's relationship with Mary Sue, being her roommate. She also didn't think that Anthony should be going out with Mary Sue. She had tried to convince Mary Sue to stop seeing Anthony before Christmas break. Now she was twisting the knife in Anthony's heart and seemed to be enjoying it.

"Why don't you shut-up and get the hell out of here," Don yelled at her.

Anthony looked at the ground, stunned by the news. He had thought many things could happen in Hilland over the break, but an engagement never entered his mind. Don didn't know what to say to him, so he just pushed him past Shelley and up the path. They walked in silence all the way back to their dorm.

On the third floor, all the girls were in the hallway talking about Mary Sue's engagement. It was what most girls hoped would happen to them sooner or later. Meet the right guy, get married, start a career, start a family—fulfill their destiny. Don guided Anthony past the girls' wing toward their room, but Anthony stopped and glanced up the hallway and saw Mary Sue. She was surrounded by well-wishers, who were giddy about her news and eager to see her new engagement ring. For a brief moment their eyes met, and Mary Sue could tell in an instant that Anthony knew, and the smile faded on her face.

MARY SUE TALKING TO THE READER...

"This is the worst. This is not how I wanted Anthony to find out. When Jim proposed to me on Christmas Eve, I called Shelley and Anita with the news. I tried to get back to the dorms early enough to be able to tell Anthony before everyone else found out about it. I didn't know what I was going to say, or how I was going to say it, but I wanted to tell him face-to-face. I owed him that much. I could see the look on his face just now."

Anthony sat on the edge of his bed staring at nothing. Don didn't know what to say, so for the moment, he let Anthony brood.

Mulling it over in his mind, he thought that for the first time in his life, he was the "bad boy." He was the "other man" in a girl's life. However, to him, he felt like he was the one who had been cheated. He had real feelings and thought he had made a real connection with Mary Sue. The relationship felt deeper and all-encompassing compared to his juvenile romantic high school relationships. He hadn't felt like "the other guy." He had felt like, "the guy."

After a half hour or so, Don couldn't stand it any longer. "Get your shit in gear, man! Come on, let's get out of here. Let's go into the forest."

Anthony shook his head, but Don would have none of it. The pair walked down the stairs. Halfway down, they met the Banshee Sisters on their way up. Don was ready to rip into them if they teased Anthony, but they were uncharacteristically quiet. As Don and Anthony passed them in the stairwell, Natalie gently put her hand on Anthony's shoulder for just an instant—an empathetic gesture. She either knew it was best to say nothing or she didn't know what to say. Lena just paused respectfully. Anthony did not break stride nor was he very aware of what happened—still numb from the morning's events.

Don and Anthony headed down the path, and down the stairs, through the apartment parking lot to the trailhead. The grey cloud cover from yesterday still kept the sun hidden from view. There were no thin shafts of light coming through the canopy above—just a grey, gloomy damp forest that matched their mood. After a short walk they paused and scrambled up a few steps onto a boulder the size of a Volkswagen Bug.

"I figure if you get suicidal and jump, you'll only bruise yourself at the bottom," Don said trying to inject some humor into the situation.

"You're always thinking of me man, and I appreciate that," Anthony joked.

"Hey, that's what roommates are for."

They sat awhile in silence, then Don pontificated, "I think you should...make the first move. You should talk to her. Right now, she doesn't know what to say. You be 'the man' and let her off the hook. I mean, what else are you going to do? You could keep trying to get her back, but what would that do. If you succeed, you have literally broken up someone else's marriage—not cool. If you fail, you look pathetic. Only Benjamin Braddock can pull that shit off like at the end of, 'The Graduate.' Get her alone, away from her little coven of witches on third floor. Talk to her in private. By the way, what'd you do to piss off Shelley and Anita? They sure seemed to be enjoying your predicament."

"I have no idea—really. Yeah, I'll try and do that the next chance I get."

"And don't get choked up or anything sentimental. Otherwise, you'll convince her she made the right decision to dump your sorry ass. I'd just say, 'Congrats on your engagement' and walk away."

Don reached in his pocket and took out a joint. From his other pocket he retrieved a blue Bic lighter. Holding the joint in his lips, he took a drag as the flame lit the end of the joint. He took another hit, then passed the joint to Anthony. In his despair, Anthony took the joint awkwardly in one hand and raised it to his lips. Taking a drag, he had burning smoke enter his nostrils and lungs at the same time. He coughed convulsively dropping the roach, which bounced off the boulder and on to the pine needle trail which then started to smolder. Anthony meanwhile, still hacking and coughing, fell from the boulder, landing flat on his back on top of the smoldering fire—putting it out. Getting up quickly, he checked the back of his shirt to make sure he wasn't still on fire.

Don looked on in amazement. "Man, Buster Keaton could not have done it any better than that." He hopped off the boulder, bent down and picked up the joint. Relighting it, he took another drag and the pair continued their hike, taking the long way around back to the campus.

Don and Anthony strolled through the forest, Don appreciating the surroundings and the pretty good dope he had scored. Anthony enjoyed the scenery and could somewhat appreciate the whiffs of cannabis he occasionally got from Don's joint.

Feeling somewhat better about life in general, the two emerged from the woods and on to the campus proper. Crossing behind Founders Hall they approached their dorm only to hear a stereo belting out a song from Side Two of Linda Ronstadt's new album, "Heart Like A Wheel".

"I've been cheated, been mistreated. When will I-I be loved," Linda crooned.

Don shook his head and said to Anthony, "If you didn't have bad luck, you wouldn't have any luck at all."

Anthony looked down and took a deep breath and continued back to the dorm.

CHAPTER 17
A New Start

Monday was a busy day as students continued to return to campus and worked on completing their class schedules for the second semester. Classes that were full and classes that were canceled added to the frustration of the time-consuming process.

Anthony and Don worked on their schedules and finally got the classes that they needed. Anthony was looking forward to Personnel Management and Psychology, but dreading Math 153. His fun class was Archery on Wednesday afternoon at 1 p.m. All through high school, his mom advised him to always have one "fun" class on his schedule. Although he was taking college prep classes in high school, he always had one art class, ceramics class, or bachelor foods cooking class in his schedule.

Next came the textbooks. He made a few bucks selling back the textbooks from first semester, but he needed to buy new ones for his upcoming classes. The bookstore was a zoo. He realized that he was taking a chance buying the textbooks before going to the first class. Sometimes professors would say you could buy the textbooks if you wanted, but it wasn't mandatory. The ones who wrote the book always required it. If you waited for the first class meeting and found out the book was mandatory, they might be out of them at the bookstore, and you wouldn't be able to do the reading until partway through the semester.

Anthony was glad he had things to keep him busy. Once his schedule was set, he walked down to the bookstore and got in a line of people that wrapped around the building. Working his way up and through the door, he finally made it to one of the folding tables and told the bewildered student-worker what books he needed. She walked back into the bowels of the stockroom and a few minutes later came back with all but one of the books he needed. The psych book was on back order and would be in next week. Good enough. He proceeded to the checkout line and paid for everything.

As he turned after putting his change away and grabbing his books, he ran right into Mary Sue. She had a load of books in her arms and was ready to pay for them. Slightly exasperated, she set them down and turned to him, "Can you wait a second? I'd like to talk to you."

Anthony nodded as she completed the transaction. They walked out together and sat on the concrete edge of a planter outside the bookstore. She held her books on her lap, almost as if she were using them to protect herself.

"You know, I didn't want things to turn out like it did. I wanted to be the one to tell you personally. I didn't want you to hear it from somebody else."

Anthony made big eyes insinuating that it didn't work out that way.

"I know, I know. I told you at the beginning of the school year, that I thought that my destiny was set. But you came along and made me think about a lot of things. You let me see that there were other possibilities, other choices, and other people. I could never have explored those possibilities without you. I have made my decision, but it wasn't a pre-determined one. It was one I made based on things you made me think about. You let me breathe when I felt like I couldn't. I know that doesn't make much sense, and it doesn't make this any easier for you. I am so sorry to have put you through this. I don't think I was very good for you, because I see that I have hurt you; but you were very good for me at this point in my life. And for that, I will always be grateful." Her voice was quaking and tears were running down her cheeks as she finished speaking.

Anthony stood up, bowed slightly, and said, "Congratulations. I am happy for you. I really am." And with that, he picked up his books and walked away. He did not want her to see his eyes welling up with tears. Don would be so pissed at him.

———————

After that, Anthony and Mary Sue seldom spoke. Relationships have life spans. Some are as long as the life span of a giant tortoise. Other relationships last as long as the life of a fruit fly. Anthony and Mary's relationship was over. Although Mary Sue would have liked to still be friends; that was too difficult a "down-shift" for Anthony's social transmission to handle. Still, on the rare occasion when they would cross paths in the dorm or on campus, they would make eye contact and nod. Both of them probably wishing for more; and both equally sad that nothing more transpired. After many weeks, half smiles shared between them were as good as it was going to be. And it stayed that way for most of what was left of the school year.

On Wednesday, class started and everyone had to get into a new routine of classes, studying and having fun.

At the inside corner of the L-shaped dorm building, on the third floor was the room of Kathy Northwood. She had a gregarious personality—always laughing and joking. The boys did not intimidate her; in fact, she enjoyed hanging out with them. Her window was ninety degrees adjacent to the window of the small study lounge in the first room of the boys' wing. One evening, she was in her dorm room studying or talking to someone on the phone...or both. Her window was open as was the window to the little study lounge. (None of the windows in the dorms had screens) Anthony was in the study lounge and decided to do something very foolish and dangerous.

Anthony enjoyed pranks. When he was younger, there was a newspaper article about how students came to school at a nearby high school only to find a tire inner tube with the words "Class of 1966" painted on it on top of the steeple of their bell tower. No one ever came forward to say who did it or how they did it. It remains a mystery and one of the best pranks ever. It took a hook-and-ladder fire truck from another city to remove the tire from the steeple.

While Anthony was pretty naïve, he was willing to take social risks in order to be funny or get attention. Being down a bit lately, he thought a good prank seemed like a good idea.

Anthony had a set of rules he followed for pranks:

1. No one can be even slightly injured by the prank.
2. No property can be destroyed by the prank
3. The prank cannot be gross or sick.
4. The prank must be thought of as witty or clever.

Bending rule number one a bit, he stepped out of the study lounge window and into the window to Kathy's room—both three stories up and above a concrete entryway.

"Oh my god!" she cried out. "This guy just stepped through my window," she told someone on the phone. "And we are on the THIRD floor," she exclaimed.

"Hi, my name is Anthony," he said as he shook her hand and stepped from the windowsill to the table by the window, then to a chair and on to the floor. "I don't believe we've met."

She shook his hand, but her mouth was still open in amazement.

"I gotta go. I'll call you back," then she squealed, "I KNOW!" and hung up the phone.

Still laughing, she said, "Pleased to meet you, I'm Kathy," faking an air of politeness. "You blew me away. So you're that guy that people are talking about?"

Anthony lowered his head in mock sadness.

Going on she said, "The one who made the nice touchdown catch in "The Big Game." I saw that. Nice job. What brings you to my room today?"

"Well, I was just in the neighborhood and thought it would be the neighborly thing to do."

"Any time. But please, next time, please use the door. You scared the hell out of me!"

Anthony poked his head out the window and looked down three stories to the concrete below and said, "It scared the hell out of me too." They talked for a while and then Anthony got up to leave and walked out her door and not her window and returned to his room. He was pleased that he had made Kathy laugh. They became good friends and commiserated with each other about relationships. Kathy was very close to a very interesting guy named Dylan who lived on third floor with Tyrone. Dylan was sensitive and cared very much how everyone was doing. He had dark, kind of long hair, and wore dark rimmed glasses. Many people sought Dylan's advice. He was a good counselor and people trusted him.

CHAPTER 18
Bro

Anthony got out of his math class at about 10 a.m. on Thursday. He headed back to the dorms to see if Don wanted to beat the crowd and go down to lunch in the dining hall a little early. He walked across campus enjoying the activity all around him. When he got to the dorm, he went up the stairs, and heard yelling and laughter. He turned left into his hallway and walked through the open door of his room following the noise. Don was sitting in his chair laughing. Randall was sitting on the edge of Anthony's bed facing Don. Keisha was sitting on Randall's lap with her arm around his neck and her feet on the bed—and she was giving Don a particularly bad time—all in good fun.

"An' you be actin' all bad because you be Italian an' stuff. Well, whatta 'bout yo name, DON! Whatta you like, "The Godfatha" in that movie—Don Cannoli o' sumpin?"

Don was laughing hard now. Once Keisha got started, she was hard to stop. Even though she normally spoke very proper English, she loved to slip into her black dialect—especially when teasing white people.

Keisha turned and saw Anthony walk in and immediately started in on him. "And Don, why you call yo white roomie, 'Bro'? That means, 'brotha' and you ain't a brotha' and his skinny white ass sure ain't a brotha'. I mean, whatz up wid dat shit?"

Anthony laughed good-naturedly as did Randall, but Don's face melted into a serious look. "You'll never know," he said gravely.

Keisha, being perceptive, knew she had said something wrong—but didn't know what it was.

Anthony picked up on it too. He didn't know why Don had called him Bro on many occasions but had never bothered to ask.

Keisha, wanting to get the laughter going again, turned to Anthony. "And you! What's with des art posters on your wall?" She waved her other arm at them. "I mean, you some kind of gay art collector or sumpin'? Let's see, what does dis shit all mean? Don Quixote—you on some crazy adventure?"

Everyone was laughing again, including Don. Keisha kept the momentum going and pressed her advantage. "A painting of a bridge—you goin' someplace? Someone handin' flowers to someone else—you lookin' fo' LOVE?"

An immediate hush fell over the room as everyone looked at Anthony. Had Keisha stepped on someone else's toes? Was it too soon after the breakup with Mary Sue to be joking about it? Everyone was waiting to see Anthony's reaction.

"I see you're getting a C+ in Psych 101," Anthony responded, rolling with the punches.

"I am NOT, you racist pig. I am gettin' a solid B! Come on Randall, let's go back to your room and study," she said in mock indignation. "If they can't appreciate my humor, it's their loss," she said the last sentence with perfect pronunciation and no hint of any dialect.

She marched out of the room holding Randall's hand, keeping him in tow. Anthony and Don continued to laugh as they heard Keisha carrying on all the way down the hallway.

"So, what was that about?" Anthony pressed Don.

A dark gloom came over Don's face. Something was weighing on Anthony's roommate. Slowly, as if it were physically painful to speak at all, Don started.

"Nobody knows, but two years ago my brother was killed in a car accident. A drunk driver killed him and his friend. Joe was just getting out of wrestling practice at 5 o'clock and I was supposed to go pick him up because I had just gotten my license. My folks thought it would be good practice for me to drive to and from school—a route which I was very familiar with—to get some driving experience. I told my mom I would get him but I had left the house early to visit a friend. We were listening to records and watching TV and I had lost track of time. At 5:20, I realized I was late and hurried to school to get him.

"He had come out and waited a bit, then one of the other, older wrestlers had offered him a ride home in his car. They were six blocks from school when they were hit broadside on the passenger door. Joe was killed instantly.

"I pulled up at the school and when I didn't see my brother, I asked the other guys coming out of the locker room where he was. They said he had waited but had gotten a ride home with someone else. I didn't think anything of it.

"When I got home, I wondered why Joe wasn't home yet. I figured he and the other guy stopped for something to eat. A little while later, a cop came to the door. When mom opened the door, the cop said something like, 'I have some bad news about Joe.' My mom understood and realized what he was saying in an instant. And she collapsed on the floor in a kneeling position but with her head on the floor. It was as if every bone in her body had instantly dissolved—like the witch melting in The Wizard of Oz. She kept saying, 'I can't breathe, I can't breathe.' Then she couldn't stop crying. I tried to comfort her. My dad tried to comfort her. When we tried to walk her back to her room to lie down, she slammed her hand against the statue of Jesus we have on a little shelf in the hallway. The statue went one way; the holy candle went the other way, both shattering into a million pieces on the floor.

"I know that it was the fault of the drunk driver. But I let him down. He was counting on me but I let him down. Some things you carry with you your whole life. I will carry this guilt for my whole life and into the next life. If I had been responsible, my Bro would still be alive today."

Together, Don and Anthony sat in silence in their dorm room for quite some time.

CHAPTER 19
Frat Party

Friday, Don and Anthony were trying to figure out what they were going to do that night.

"We aren't stayin' around this dump tonight. How about if we go to the Forest Fern Complex and watch a movie? They are supposed to show some old movie and it is only a quarter to get in. You can't beat a price like that."

"Sure, sounds great. Let's do it," Anthony replied.

Early that evening, they headed to the dining hall for dinner and then planned to hang around for the movie. After a "Fish Sticks Friday" dinner with French fries, the pair headed downstairs to the multi-purpose room which this evening was serving as the movie theater. The Banshee Sisters were already in line. As they walked up, Anthony's face fell.

"What's the matter Bro?" Don scanned the area quickly like a Secret Service agent. He didn't see Mary Sue, so he was a bit confused.

"Look at what movie is showing."

"Casablanca," Don answered as he looked at the movie poster on the wall. He still did not get the connection. Only after a few seconds, he said, "Oh. Not a good choice. 'Movie's about a lost love. Bummer. Come on; let's get out of here 'Rick,'" referring to Humphrey Bogart's character. "We'll go to a party at the frat house that I heard about."

With that, they got out of line and started walking to town. Natalie turned to look their way and saw them leaving. Her smile disappeared and she turned back around.

Don and Anthony walked across the bridge over Highway 101 and into town. Instead of turning left towards the town square, they turned right towards the residential area where there were houses and apartments. A few blocks down, loud music could be heard coming from an old dilapidated Victorian house. A geeky kid with granny glasses was standing at the gate talking to a few girls—who seemed to be a bit bored and wanted to get inside to the party. They were decked out in party attire and colorful high heel shoes.

Knowing he wasn't a fraternity member, Don needed to B.S. this guy into letting them both into the party.

"Where's the party at?" Don asked in a friendly manner.

Looking the pair over from head to toe, the gatekeeper said in a condescending way, "Never end a sentence with a preposition."

"Okay. Where's the party at ASSHOLE?" the now slightly pissed-off Don said, rephrasing it.

The girls laughed out loud, and Don pushed his way past the gatekeeper with Anthony following behind him. "Hey, wait, you guys aren't members!" he yelled.

"Stan's a friend of mine," Don replied. "He invited us." The girls, anxious to get into the party, ran to catch up with Don. He walked into the party with a girl on each arm. A third girl hung back and walked in with Anthony.

Once inside the door, Anthony shouted over the din of the throbbing music, "You know someone in the fraternity?"

"Hell no. I just figure a guy like that doesn't have any friends so he wouldn't know if there was a Stan in the fraternity or not."

Brilliant, Anthony thought to himself.

The frat brothers were considering telling Don and Anthony to beat it because they knew they weren't members, but it appeared that they brought some good-looking girls with them, so they decided not to kick them out. Don grabbed a beer out of an ice chest by the door and handed it to Anthony and grabbed another one for himself. The girls were giddy with excitement and were soon the center of attention. The girl that walked in with Anthony tried striking up a conversation with him but the music on the stereo was too loud, so they went into the backyard.

A spotlight on the back of the house illuminated the dead lawn and tall weeds along the fence in the backyard. Many people were sitting on old patio furniture in small groups, laughing and talking. A few small groups in the shadowed corners of the yard were bent over with a small glowing light being handed back and forth between them.

"I'm Sharon," the girl said introducing herself to Anthony.

"Hey, I'm Anthony."

"Do you go to State?"

"Yes. How about you?"

"I go to Coastal Community College down the road from here. I plan on transferring up here next term. Do you like it?"

"It's pretty good. I may transfer to Southwestern State next term. I'm not sure yet."

Don walked up, handing Anthony another beer and asked, "How's it going? Making some new friends?" Sharon smiled. Don nodded, then walked away and went up to a frat brother in the yard and struck up a conversation. They talked for a while then both of them went back into the house. Following the frat brother upstairs, they both entered a room and closed the door. Thirty minutes later, Don came out and adjusted a package he had slipped in the back of his pants under his jacket.

Going downstairs and out the back door, Don was looking for Anthony who was on his third beer. He was listening to Sharon who was still doing most of the talking. As Don approached the pair, Anthony hunched over and puked on Sharon's bright red heels.

Don was shocked, but not as shocked as Sharon. She just stared at her shoes and the vomit splattered on them. Don bent down and removed her heels. He ran over to the garden hose near the back steps of the house and hosed them off. He ran back and like Prince Charming putting the glass slipper on Cinderella, he bent down and put the red heels back on an appreciative Sharon. Turning to Anthony, he said, "Come on Bro. Time to go home."

Don adjusted the package under the back of his jacket and then helped Anthony to his feet. "I can't believe you puked after only three beers."

"I'm not used to drinking beer," he slurred.

Out of the old Victorian house and across the bridge back towards the dorm, Don helped a staggering Anthony along. When they were a hundred yards from the dorm a bright light froze them in space. A campus cop sitting in his patrol car had turned his spotlight on them.

"What's going on here gentlemen?" the cop asked.

"My friend here was studying in the library until late and is totally exhausted. I am just helping him back to the dorm so he can get some rest."

Anthony added slurring his words, "I can't believe I puked on her shoes."

"So, tell me another one," the cop said sarcastically.

"Okay, he's my roommate and he had too much to drink. God's honest truth."

"He didn't drink a whole bottle of whiskey and is going to end up having his stomach pumped, is he?"

Don left Anthony slumped at the curb for a moment and approached the cop. "I swear, he only had three beers. I think he'll be okay. We're almost back to our dorm. I swear I will take care of him."

"Okay, but make sure he doesn't puke on campus," the cop said excusing them. He turned off the spotlight, started the car and drove off to continue his patrol.

Don nervously adjusted the package under his jacket and helped Anthony to his feet. They zigzagged a bit but finally got back to the dorm, up the stairs, and to their room. As Don flopped Anthony on his bed, he whispered, "Good-night Bro."

Anthony slept soundly that night and did not throw-up again. The next morning, he woke up with a terrible headache and made a blood oath to never drink again.

CHAPTER 20
Viva Roma

Anthony was not one to brood—at least not longer than several weeks. Although it probably wasn't true, Anthony felt like when he walked down the hallways in the dorm, conversations between groups of people would stop as he walked by them. He likened it to people on sidewalks standing silently as a hearse drove past them. He didn't know if they felt sorry for him for being dumped or if they thought that he must be damaged goods—"something must be wrong if it didn't work out with a nice girl like Mary Sue." Or did they just think he was emotionally fragile and were being careful around him. He definitely felt like some people were treating him as if he were made of glass.

"Hey Heart-broken, do you wanna go to the old movie marathon in the Complex next week?" Natalie was not one of those people. Maybe it was the Italian in her that let her say whatever was on her mind.

"What?" Anthony replied somewhat taken back.

"Do – you – want – to – go – to – the – movies – with – me – next – week?" she said exaggerating her clear pronunciation. "And if you say 'no', I am going to hit you in the face with my softball mitt again."

Anthony reacted by covering his nose with one hand, lest she be armed with the mitt and said, "Sure. You want me to pick you up or shall I meet you there?"

"Come and get me," she said as she smiled at her own slightly suggestive double-entendre. "It starts at 7." She turned and headed for her room.

"I'll see you at a quarter till," Anthony called after her. *Wow*, he thought to himself. This is a strange, but good turn of events. He decided to take a mature approach to this budding relationship. No more childish antics. It was time to act like an adult. He decided to pass a note to Lena.

"Meet me in the quad in five minutes," it read. Anthony casually walked down the girls' hallway keeping an eye out so he could avoid both Natalie and Mary Sue, but for completely different reasons. He saw Lena talking to another girl a few doors down from her and Natalie's room, which was perfect. He approached and casually pressed the note into Lena's hand as he walked by her. She was somewhat confused and looked back at him as he headed for the far stairway. Then she read the note. She looked back again, but Anthony was already gone, as he was heading for the quad.

Finding a bench, Anthony sat down and waited. The quad seemed to be held in the hands of the two L-shaped dorms. It was a refuge from the rest of the campus, with its trees and shrubs, benches, grass area, and patio. Few other students from the campus would intrude into the sanctuary of the dorm residents. While it was a place to study or to take a break from studying, it was actually within view of half of the population of the two dorm buildings. Still, in the quad, one could look up and see dozens of open windows, some with curtains blowing in the breeze...yet few people actually looking down on it. It was as if all the dorm residents respected the intimacy and solitude of their little oasis, as if they understood the need to escape from the close quarters of dorm living—the drama, the noise, and the people.

Soon, Lena came out of the stairway door at the far end of the building. She was smiling and scooted quickly over towards Anthony, walking something like a female Charlie Chaplin.

"I haven't been passed a note since fifth grade!" she said excitedly. "What's going on?" she said as she sat on the bench next to him.

"Nothing big. Natalie just asked me to go the movie marathon next week. I was a bit surprised and wondered what to make of all of it."

Lena giggled and slapped Anthony's knee. "She told me she was going to ask you out. She said you'd never be smart enough to figure out that she liked you. Did you know that? She has liked you since the beginning of the year. Why do you think we ransacked your room that time? That was her idea. This is so exciting!"

Lena, who was a beauty in her own right, also had an effervescent personality—and it was bubbling all over the place right now.

"Okay, okay," Anthony said trying to calm her down a bit. "Well, tell me a little bit about her. I don't know anything about her other than I think she plays softball."

"Well, like I said, she likes you. She doesn't see why you were interested in Mary Sue. She thought it was wrong of her to be interested in you if she knew she was going to be engaged to that other guy back home."

"Okay. Question number one," Anthony started his questioning. "Does she have a boyfriend back home? I don't want to make the same mistake twice."

"There is a guy back home that kind of liked her, but she wasn't interested in him," she responded. "They were never boyfriend and girlfriend and they never went out on a date."

"And you two, aren't...you know—interested in each other that way?" he put extra emphasis on "that." Some people had suspected as much.

135

Lena laughed and she slapped his knee again. "No, we're just crazy good friends. Do people think that about us? That's funny. Let them think what they want. How about you? Do you like her?"

"Of course, I do. She's cute and has a sense of humor I suppose. I didn't know she liked me. In fact, I kind of thought she disliked me, with the ransacking and hitting me with the mitt."

"If she disliked you, she would have hit you with a bat and not a mitt. You know she has three brothers. She is a bit of a Tom Boy. I think it came from trying to keep up with them," Lena continued. "And trust me, she likes you. She thought it was hilarious that you just sat there and watched us tear up your room. Most people would have freaked out. You were so cool and she liked that."

"Cool?" Anthony exclaimed! "I was in shock!"

Lena laughed again, this time giving Anthony a shove that almost knocked him off the bench. Both of the Banshee Sisters were definitely into physical comedy.

"So is there anything else I can tell you?" she asked.

"No, that's it. I just wanted to make sure I wasn't getting into another bad situation. Thanks for coming down here and talking to me."

"No problem. You are going to have fun at the movie thing next week." Lena got up to leave but turned back for a second. "And if you hurt her, I will beat you up and her brothers will kill you. Have fun!" Her last sentence was strangely gleeful compared the ominous tone of the previous one.

Nothing is easy, Anthony thought to himself. He got up from the bench and went up the main stairway to his room. As he passed Tyrone and Dylan's room, he saw a small group of guys sitting around talking—so Anthony walked in and sat down trying to catch what the conversation was all about.

"Well, you know this is Big Foot country up here," Tyrone explained to the group. "And I think it would be a great prank!"

Dylan countered, "But where are we going to get a gorilla suit?"

Anthony, quite confused asked, "What are you guys talking about? Big Foot? Gorilla suit? It sounds crazy. But I love it!"

Randall summarized for him. "We wanted to get Hector to dress up in a gorilla costume and right at sunset, have him carry Lisa, that tiny chick from second floor, I think she is a gymnast, and take her into the woods. We'd tell her to scream and stuff. People would think it was a Big Foot abduction—or a gymnast abduction by a Big Foot. The only problem is that we don't know where we could get a gorilla costume and we probably couldn't afford to rent one even if we found one."

Everyone sat around for a long moment in silence as the wheels were turning. These were four, fairly intelligent and imaginative college students. They would come up with something.

"I think we should think white," said Dylan.

"Say WHAT?" shrieked Tyrone.

"We should think white, you know, like the Abominable Snowman," stated Dylan.

Randall said disgustedly, "So since we can't find a gorilla suit, we'll just get a Abominable Snowman suit?"

"Hey, I'm just brain-storming here," Dylan said defending himself.

Tyrone had a thought, "yeah, yeah. Maybe we could find an old white shag rug somewhere and use that to make a costume."

Silence again. Everyone looked at each other for a spark of inventiveness.

Anthony started slowly, "Remember how everyone was into streaking a year or two ago?'"

"Like the guy at the Academy Awards last year?" recalled Randall.

"Yeah, yeah. Like that!"

"You want Hector to streak?" asked Tyrone with a disgusted look on his face.

Everyone groaned.

"No," Anthony went on, making it up as he went. "We make him the Abominable Streaker, like the abominable snowman. We cover him in white. White shaving cream. Head to toe."

"What about Lisa?"

"We don't need her. We just run the Abominable Streaker through the other dorm...just the girls' hallways. We'll scare the hell out of them. It will be great!"

Randall said, "I like it. It is simple, devious, and cheap. Let's go ask Hector."

"No freaking way." Hector seemed dead set against it. The foursome had tracked him down in the hallway.

"Ah come on, it will be fun! We'll scare the hell out of them!" Randall said trying to convince him.

"No-Freaking-Way!" Hector repeated more forcefully, then walked away.

138

Tyrone, Dylan, Randall and Anthony all looked at each other. Then Randall had an epiphany. "We don't need Hector. We don't need him because the Abominable Streaker isn't carrying Lisa anymore. One of us can do it."

"Oh no!" said Tyrone. "A naked black man running across campus, mmmm-mmm. Not good. I don't want no part of that one. Trouble written all over that."

Dylan seemed to shy away from the idea also. "I don't think I could do that. It's just not me. Besides, if I get caught..." He didn't finish the sentence.

Randall and Anthony just looked at each other. "It's you or me," said Randall. Let's flip for it. Winner does it. The other three of us help. You call it."

"You're on," Anthony said seemingly up for the challenge.

Still standing in the hallway with the others, Randall reached in his pocket and pulled out a quarter that was destined for the laundry room, but now it had a much more important role. Randall flipped the coin high in the air.

"Tails," Anthony called.

CHAPTER 21
A Flip of the Coin

Lena raced back up the stairs to their room to tell Natalie what Anthony had said. They sat on her bed and Lena gave her all the details, then they laughed and giggled like schoolgirls—which of course is what they were. Natalie was pleased that Anthony was looking forward to their movie night. She knew her straightforward, brutally honest approach was not always appreciated although it always seemed to work with her three brothers.

Natalie started thinking about what she might wear on their date. Ultimately her ensemble would revolve around bib overalls. She started to think more on it when she realized that her English class was about to begin. So, she grabbed her books, said good-bye to Lena and sprinted down the hallway towards the stairs.

Lena smiled thinking about Natalie's upcoming date. She felt fortunate that she had been paired up as roommates with Natalie. Although they both had similar, unfettered personalities, they were from completely different backgrounds.

Natalie had been born and raised in Ventura, not far from the beach. Most of her life she had run around barefoot and always had sandy feet. The only time she wore shoes was while attending Catholic grade school and high school. The nuns would have none of her kicking off her shoes—both figuratively and literally.

While she loved her brothers, the two older ones did nothing to help develop her feminine side. They did however teach her the art of baseball; skills which she applied to softball. She excelled in hitting, throwing and catching. And it was the only time she enjoyed wearing anything on her feet—that being her cleats. She was the Most Valuable Player on her high school softball team.

Patrick, Natalie's younger brother was not very athletic, and seemed more sensitive. He enjoyed reading books and listening to classical music. Even though Natalie and Patrick shared little common interests, Natalie was very protective of him— sometimes from her masculine older brothers who would give Patrick a bad time; or from kids at school who would sometimes pick on him for not wanting to join in their games or rough-housing.

Lena on the other hand was an only child. She was born in Minnesota, but her parents moved to Stockton, California when she was still very young. Her parents are both Filipino, her father being a physician and her mother, a librarian. She too went to Catholic school although her schools' demographics were far different than Natalie's. Lena's classmates were mainly the children of migrant farm workers and first-generation American citizens. She was practically bilingual, learning both English and Spanish as a small child. Probably from her parents' desire to immerse themselves in American culture, their whole family enjoyed watching baseball on television or occasionally going to a Giants game in San Francisco. From this exposure, Lena developed her interest in softball and was one of the most talented players on her high school team.

Both girls had been recruited to play softball at Sequoia State, although it is a non-scholarship sport. They were fortunate enough to have been assigned the same dorm room and had gotten along well right from the start. Lena considered Natalie her new best friend and the feeling was reciprocated.

Randall caught the quarter in his left hand and flipped it over on to the back of his right hand. Pulling his left hand away, he uncovered the coin and showing the other three guys.

"Tails never fails!" Anthony proclaimed with a smile. "We do it tonight!"

At 9 p.m., the quartet met in the restrooms. Anthony stripped down and went to his locker and grabbed an athletic supporter and stepped into it. Tyrone protested, "Man, what are you doing? You are supposed to be a streaker. You can't wear a jock!"

"You wanna go instead?"

"Nope."

"With the shaving cream on, no one will notice," Anthony explained.

Tyrone looked at Randall. "Would you go buck naked?"

"I don't know. I think Anthony is right," answered Randall.

Dylan chimed in, "That's a good point. If he gets caught, that might be a key issue. I know. I am pre-law."

"Okay, let's do it," said Anthony. "You guys do my back and head. I'll do my private areas. I don't want any of you touching my tool kit. We gotta work fast so the foam doesn't go flat. Grab your shaving cream cans."

They all went to their lockers and came back with four different brands of shaving cream. They all looked at each other, then they went to work. The cans swished out a steady stream of foam and they quickly covered him from head to toe.

142

They were all laughing their asses off by the time they were finished. Randall stood back to see if there was any skin left uncovered on Anthony's body. "Looks good!" he said.

Just then Don walked into the restroom and was stunned. "What the hell?"

"How does he look?" asked Randall.

"Amazing," a dumbfounded Don replied. Anthony silently did a slow three hundred sixty degree turn. "Who is it?" Don asked. The foursome burst into laughter.

"Don, it's me," Anthony finally spoke.

"Wow. You're a messed-up dude," replied Don, shaking his head.

With that Anthony walked out into the hallway, and in a few seconds, all the guys present were laughing and cheering. Randall led Tyrone, Dylan and Don over to his room that faced the quad so they could watch from his window.

First Anthony jogged through the third-floor girls' wing and howled like a wolf. The girls shrieked with laughter. No one knew who it was, and Anthony was happy about that. He got to the end of the hallway and pressed the push bar to open it. His feet slid a bit when he stepped on to the slick cement floor of the landing because his feet were covered with shaving cream. He jogged carefully down the stairs, out the door and over to the doorway of the rival dorm. He could feel his heart pounding with excitement. A girl was just coming out of the door when Anthony past her going the opposite direction.

"There he goes!" Randall said to the other three observers, all of them peering out of the windows. Once inside the hallway, Anthony let out a blood-curdling scream and jogged down the hallway. The four observers saw the girls in the rooms that faced the quad, leap off their beds or away from their desks and open their doors to look into the hallway. They could tell Anthony's location through the hallway by which girls were running to their doors. First, the girls in the rooms on the right ran to their doors, and then the middle rooms, then the rooms on the left.

"And he should now be entering the lobby and lounge area," Tyrone said as if he was giving the group an update of what was obvious. But nothing seemed to be happening in the entry to the lobby.

"Maybe he went up the stairs to the girls' hallway on the second floor," Dylan hypothesized. But none of the girls they could see through the second-floor windows were reacting at all. They all looked at each other.

Finally, the Abominable Streaker appeared, sprinting out of the main entrance to the lobby and running diagonally across the quad. He was still howling like a wolf and people from both dorms whose windows faced the quad, were all peering out in amazement. Some were cheering, some were applauding. Randall, Tyrone, Dylan, and Don were all cheering like their team just won the World Series. They ran back out of the room and sprinted to the end of the hall where Anthony would appear. Finally, Anthony came sprinting through the door and ran right to the restroom and sat down on a bench—completely out of breath.

"That was amazing, man!" Tyrone exclaimed.

"Hilarious!" Randall added.

"What happened though? You were completely off the radar when we thought you should be in the lobby," Dylan asked.

"I know. I was doing fine," started Anthony, still having to pause between gasps of air. "The whole way, either someone was coming through the door the other way, the door was propped open, or there was a push bar I could press to open the door."

"So?" Dylan asked impatiently.

Gulping for a breath, Anthony continued. "As I jogged down the hallway, the girls were freaking out. It was great. I kept spreading the shaving cream around to make sure I was completely covered, so it was all over my hands."

Another pause for air.

"When I got to the end of the hallway, I went to open the door and I couldn't because it wasn't a push bar. It was a shiny brass doorknob and when I grabbed it, I had no grip at all. My hand just slid around it. I even tried using two hands, but still nothing. I was literally trapped!"

"So then what happened," they all asked in unison.

Now slightly recovered, Anthony continued, "Well, I turn around and all these girls were coming out of their rooms from both sides of the hallway. At first, they were scared and screaming and stuff. Then, when they see I'm trapped at the end of the hallway, one girl yells out, 'Let's get him!' It was terrifying man! One girl had a chair, another a wine bottle, another picked up a baseball bat."

The four were now listening with bated breath.

"When they were just about to attack, a girl came through the door the other way. Thank God! I sort of nudged her out of the way and sprinted all the way back here. I saw my life pass before my eyes! It was crazy!"

Now all of them, including Anthony were laughing hysterically. It was a great prank and people would be talking about it for a while.

"Now remember," Randall reminded everyone, "not a word about this to anyone. It is the rule of Omertá. The longer it is a secret, the longer the people with speculate. We want to keep this one going a long time. Those girls will remember that for the rest of their lives."

"So will I!" Anthony said as he hit the showers.

CHAPTER 22
Not So Happy Birthday

<u>March 1975</u>

In March, the days were starting to get longer but there was still a chill in the air when Anthony left for his 10 a.m. Personnel Management class on Wednesday. He thought Don had a morning Physics class, but when Anthony left, Don was still asleep. Maybe his class had been cancelled that day. He had all the luck.

Today's lecture was on motivation. The professor was lecturing on Maslow's Hierarchy of Needs. Anthony had sketched the pyramid in his notes as the professor drew it on the chalkboard. As the professor went on, Anthony filled in the five levels of the pyramid on his paper. It actually made sense. Anthony identified himself as being on the third level—his Social Needs were being met—to some degree. The professor wrapped up his lecture around 10:50 a.m. Anthony almost felt bad as he enjoyed learning about motivation. In his mind, he was seeing it being applied to a football team. Maybe one day, he'd be a coach.

Anthony left class and crossed the campus heading back to the dorm. If Don was still there, maybe they'd go to the dining hall for his late breakfast and Anthony's early lunch. At the top of the stairs, he turned left down the hallway to their room. The door was locked, which was slightly unusual, so Anthony dug in his pocket for the key, unlocked the door and walked in.

Seeing a gun normally wouldn't alarm Anthony. His father had taught him how to shoot at a young age and had bought him a single shot .22 rifle when he was 12 years old. When he saw the revolver sitting on a towel in Don's lap, his instinctive thought was that Don might be going target shooting with the other outdoorsmen on third floor, like Hector. Those guys were always going fishing, or hiking. He figured maybe they were going hunting or something.

By his third step into the room, a wave of nausea came over Anthony as he realized the gravity of the situation. Don sat on his bed on the left side of the room. His feet were on the floor and covering his lap was a grey towel. On the towel, was a Colt Official Police Model revolver with a four-inch barrel. The blued finish of the metal and the wood-stained grips made the gun appear deceivingly beautiful and seemed to hide its sinister power. It was loaded with six rounds of .38 Special, hollow-point ammunition—a particularly deadly load. Don was only thinking about using one round.

Anthony tried to speak, but his throat was completely dry. He swallowed and tried again. "Don, what are we doing here?" Anthony asked as slowly and calmly as he could. Don said nothing but slid his right hand over and grasped the revolver while it was still in his lap. The gun was still pointed towards the window, not threatening Anthony at all. "Don, talk to me buddy."

Speaking as if he were in a trance and staring off into space, Don began, "Today is Joe's birthday. He would have been seventeen years old today."

Anthony put the pieces of the puzzle together quickly now and realized that Don was on the edge of a dangerously high cliff of his own making. If Anthony said the wrong thing, it could push Don over the edge. He walked over and closed the door to their room then went back and sat on his bed facing Don. "Where did you get this gun? You know they aren't allowed on campus."

"I know. I borrowed it from a guy at the frat party." With that, tears stared rolling down Don's normally stoic face. "I did it. He's not here because of me."

"Don, you know that's not true. It was the fault of the drunk driver. And what is this going to solve?" The word "this" had never before carried so much weight. There was perspiration on his forehead, as the tension in the room grew thick.

"I don't know, I don't know," Don repeated now looking up towards the ceiling. "The guilt is like a weight I carry around with me every day. Sometimes I can hardly breathe."

Anthony's mind was in overdrive, scrambling to find the right words to de-escalate the situation. "Don, that weight will probably never go away, but I am here to help you carry that weight." He emphasized the word, "I."

"You can't. You don't know what it is like. It is on me. I saw what it did to my mother. I saw what it did to my family." He shook his head slowly.

Anthony remembered how in class, he always grasped concepts better when they were presented by the professor in "three points."

"First, this isn't what Joe would want you to do. You know that. He doesn't blame you at all. Second, think of your mom. You told me how she reacted when she was told that Joe was killed—how it literally crushed her to the ground. You don't want to have her go through that again. No parent should have to go through something like losing a child. To have it happen twice is beyond comprehension. And third, I need you Bro. I have gone through something I have never gone through before and you were there in the foxhole with me. You got me through it."

"I don't think I can get through this. You can't help me. No one can help me. God can't even help me."

"Don, who doesn't forgive you? Who is holding you responsible for your brother's death besides you? Do your parents blame you? Did your friends blame you? Who, beside yourself, is putting the blame on you? I'll tell you who—no one. You have made yourself judge, jury and...you know."

"It is just the way it's got to be. I can't go on like this," Don replied half sobbing.

"No, it doesn't 'GOT' to be this way. YOU are making it this way," Anthony countered.

Don kept shaking his head from side to side. His thumb was stroking the hammer of the gun, not enough to cock it, but his intention was clear. Anthony's mouth was still dry as he wracked his brain for the right words to save his friends life, which was in severe danger at the moment. Trying to find another approach since everything he had said so far didn't seem to be working, Anthony weighed in again. "You feel bad because you didn't give Joe a ride home. Like you were supposed to be there to protect him. What if Joe is looking at it from the point of view that he was protecting you."

Don had a quizzical look on his face and Anthony wasn't quite sure where he was going with this. "Maybe Joe knew on some spiritual level that there was going to be a car accident on the way home and two people would be killed. Maybe that's why he didn't wait for you. He didn't want to put you in danger. Maybe he wanted to protect you from being killed. And he succeeded. You are here today...because of him. He saved you! Don't go and ruin his sacrifice. He gave it all for you."

It was the most convoluted of the many points Anthony was trying to make. Don just stared across the room at him; tears still streaming down his face; right hand still holding the revolver in his lap. But now he was nodding as if he understood.

Anthony stood up and slowly stepped towards Don. He gently and slowly reached down and put his clammy, sweaty hand around the frame of the gun. Pulling it away slowly, Don released it. Anthony pressed the cylinder release and ejected the six cartridges into his hand and set them on his bed. He pushed the cylinder back into place where it locked in the frame with an indifferent metallic snap. Pulling the towel off Don's lap, he wrapped the towel around the unloaded gun and put it in the top cabinet above his closet by his luggage. He then picked up the six cartridges off the bed and put them in his pocket. Firearm and ammunition separated—situation defused. But there was still Don who needed consoling.

Still in a daze, Don continued to sit on the bed. He looked out the window to his left and for a few moments, seemed to be in another place, or seeing another dimension. Maybe, on some level he was looking for Joe and maybe Joe told him not to feel guilty. At any rate, when he looked back at Anthony, he could tell that Don was back from wherever he had been. Don still looked exhausted and emotionally spent, but he was back from the edge of the cliff. Anthony took a deep breath and let it out slowly.

Anthony then talked to Don about getting some counseling on campus. There was a support group who were well trained in helping people like Don. He promised he would go—and Anthony promised to make sure he did.

"Man, I'd say let's go out to the rock and smoke a joint, but can we go eat first? I'm starving," Anthony said trying to lighten the mood. Don nodded and stood up slowly. The pair headed downstairs to the path to the dining hall. Along the way, when Don wasn't looking, Anthony nonchalantly tossed the six bullets in a trashcan along the path. Anthony hoped they didn't incinerate the trash on campus.

In the dining hall, Buzz made Don an order of French toast from their thick sliced, homemade cinnamon bread topped with whipped butter and warm maple syrup. Anthony ordered two cheese enchiladas with a side of refried beans. They grabbed their drinks and sat down. Surprisingly, Don ate well and cleaned his plate. Anthony ate one enchilada and a little of the refried beans. He was still dealing with what had just occurred. They had both just dodged a bullet, both figuratively and literally.

Later, Anthony planned to turn in the gun to the campus police saying he found it under a bush outside the dorm.

CHAPTER 23
Movie Night

One of the popular events on campus is the Classic Movie Marathon. It is held in the in the Forest Fern Complex and is sponsored by all the LGA's. Students bring their sleeping bag or a blanket and stretch out on the floor of the multi-purpose room. The dining hall provides sodas and popcorn throughout the night and hot chocolate, coffee and donuts in the morning. The five feature films begin at 7 p.m. on Friday night and run until 5 a.m. Saturday morning. Movies start approximately every two hours. The LGA's even have two, 16 mm movie projectors so there is no pause between reels. Both projectionists watch the screen as the movie approaches the end of one reel. It is almost like a real movie theatre except the audience is lying down instead of sitting.

That day, Anthony cruised by the bookstore after class, looking for some little gift for Natalie. They had all the t-shirts, sweatshirts, hats and pennants with the school's name on it, but that wasn't what he was looking for. Then he passed the discount bin and found a teddy bear that held a Christmas tree from the pre-holiday Christmas items. No one had bought the poor little guy and he was only three dollars. Anthony plucked him out of the bin and took him to the register. He gave the girl a five dollar-bill and she gave him his change and put the bear in a plastic bag with the school logo emblazoned on the front. So much for saving the planet.

Outside, Anthony grabbed the creature and wrestled the Christmas tree from his little arms and threw it in the trash. He straightened the red ribbon around his neck and looked him over—*Good to go,* Anthony thought to himself. He stuffed the bear back in the fossil fuel-based, plastic bag and hurried back to the dorm. He wanted to get down to dinner and then back up to the dorm to shower and get dressed for the big night, or the long night as the case may be.

As Anthony walked through the door to their room, Don was sitting at his desk studying.

"Are you going to the Movie Marathon tonight?" asked Anthony

"I've got a chemistry marathon tonight, Bro. I'm going to have to pass on this one." Don seemed focused on his work, so Anthony didn't bother inviting him down to the dining hall for dinner. Don would eat when he was hungry.

So, Anthony trotted downstairs, down the path and into the dining hall. *Thank God it wasn't Fish Stick Friday again*, Anthony thought to himself. Instead, he ate light—a salad topped with everything from the garden and New England clam chowder soup. Perfect. Devouring that, he headed back up to the dorm to shower and dress.

A half hour later Anthony was ready to go. He picked up the Christmas bear that was now just a bear from his desk. Don was still working at this desk, trying to calculate something to do with a mole, and not the underground rodent kind of mole. He was working with the kind of mole that had to do with the number of atoms in 12 grams of carbon-12. Anthony figured Don was either going to have a late dinner or no dinner at all. He didn't even interrupt Don to say good-bye but quietly left the room and closed the door behind him.

It was nice to walk into the girls' hallway without feeling self-conscious or like he was sneaking around with someone else's future wife—which of course, he had been doing with Mary Sue. Stopping by to pick up Natalie, he noticed that he just felt more comfortable and confident. He didn't know why. He made a mental note to think about that sometime later.

Knocking on the open door to their room, Anthony walked in to see both girls studying quietly at their desks. Lena turned around and smiled, then nudged Natalie as if to let her know that her date had arrived. Natalie pretended to still be engrossed in her work and did not turn around. She was going to let him wait, at least a few seconds longer—not unlike a cat playing with a mouse before eating it. Now that she knew he was interested in her, she treated him with a casual indifference that she would continue as long as he sought her affections.

When she turned around, Anthony was slightly taken back by how pretty she looked. He had not previously seen her with make-up and all the other stuff that girls wear. She looked striking. She wore the standard Sequoia State uniform of bib overalls, but with only one strap hitched in kind of a sexy look. Under that, she wore a brown and white plaid flannel shirt with several of the top buttons undone revealing her long neck and more than a hint of her firm cleavage.

Standing up she saw the proffered gift of a fake wild beast and reacted like she was more excited to see the bear than Anthony himself. *Cat playing with mouse*, he thought. She hugged the bear and placed it on the little dresser next to her bed. Then she pulled the yellow comforter off her bed and grabbed her pillow.

"I forgot my pillow and blanket," he said.

"You can share mine," she said in a very matter-of-fact way. She started dragging the comforter out the door while holding the pillow under her arm.

"Here, I'll carry the comforter for you," he said while taking it from her and gathering it up so it wouldn't drag. Together they walked down the stairs, along the path and into the Forest Fern Complex. In the Complex, the entrance to the multi-purpose room was decorated with old movie posters of the Marx Brothers, Yul Brenner, and Roy Rogers—all supposedly making appearances on the big screen this evening. The LGA's had also made primitive, construction paper movie cameras, director's chairs, and megaphones to hang on the wall in and around the posters. The whole place had a festive feel to it.

The movies wouldn't start for another half hour, but people were already staking out areas for themselves. Some wanted to be close to the movie screen so they could see it more easily while lying down. Others had brought beach chairs along with their sleeping bags or blankets. It almost looked more like a campground than a movie marathon.

"Where do you want to sit?" questioned Anthony.

"Back here," she said. "We can lean against the back wall, and if we talk a bit, we won't disturb many people." Anthony nodded and they set up camp. As they settled in, other people from the dorm were finding their places on the carpeted floor of the multi-purpose room. Anthony went over to the snack table and got a bag of freshly popped popcorn and two cans of soda. Returning, he sat down, handed a soda to Natalie, and set the bag of popcorn down between them.

"So, what did you see in Mary Sue?" she asked point blank. There is nothing subtle about Natalie.

"Hey, she was...and is still a nice person," Anthony said almost defensively.

"Then why would she get involved with you if she knew she was going to get engaged to what's-his-name back home?"

Anthony had not expected this interrogation. "I guess she wasn't sure." Wanting to change the subject,

156

Anthony countered, "How about you? Is there someone back in Ventura that you are longing for?"

"Nope. I went to a very small Catholic school and everyone knew everyone else. Almost like a family. Few people dated within the school. How about you? How big was your high school?" she asked.

"Big, close to 3000 students," he answered. "What about you? Were you the shy, quiet type in high school?"

"What?" she exclaimed. "Are you kidding? I almost got kicked out of school several times."

"Really!" Anthony laughed. "What did you do, besides hit someone in the face with a mitt, to get in trouble?"

"There was this one nun, who taught Religion class, Sister Agnes. She had my two older brothers a few years prior and they drove her crazy. So, when she found out I was their sister, she had it out for me. One day, it was supposed to be quiet time while we read a chapter from our textbook. The girl behind me asked me a question and I turned around and told her to be quiet. Well, Sister Agnes ripped into me, which was wrong, and then started in on how my brothers were so bad also. Now she was picking on my family, and that is something you should never do to an Italian family. When there is trouble, we all pull together. So finally, I stood up and gave her a piece of my mind. I think I called her a hypocrite, and some other horrible things. She sent me to the principal's office, where I told Father Doyle the entire story. He got me to admit that even though I was trying to tell the girl to be quiet, that to Sister Agnes it did look like I was breaking the rules. But then he said that he would speak to her about speaking ill of my family."

Natalie, looked away for a bit like the event still bothered her.

"So, did you get suspended or something?" asked Anthony.

"Kind of," she laughed. "For the rest of the week, I went to the principal's office instead of my Religion class. He had me sit in a chair in the corner of his office and read my Religion textbook, while he did his work or talked on the phone. The next week, I was two chapters ahead of everyone else in the class. And that's just one of the times I got in trouble. It was a good thing Father Doyle liked our family."

Anthony had no doubt every word of her story was true. Natalie seemed spirited and loyal to her family and friends.

"So do you have a car?" she asked, changing the subject.

"Yes, but I didn't bring it up to school since I was living on campus," he answered. "Why?"

"Okay, tell me what bumper stickers you have on it," she said going further. "For the last several years, everyone has some sort of bumper sticker on their car. I can tell a lot about a person by what bumper stickers they have. Like if a person has an 'America, Love it or Leave It' bumper sticker, he is definitely a conservative. If they have 'Boycott Grapes' or 'Green Peace' or 'Save the Whales', they are definitely into liberal causes. Some people are a mixture. If a person has a 'Live Better/Work Union' bumper sticker, they are probably middle-of-the-road Democrats. They probably own guns and hunt, so they are conservative on the Second Amendment. They probably support taking care of the environment, so they have a place to hunt, so that gives them a liberal slant. They belong to a union, so they support workers' rights, and they're again, a liberal."

Her oratory mesmerized Anthony. "Are you a sociology major?" he asked.

"Yes. How'd you guess?" she smiled.

"Well, I think I just heard the introduction to your Master's Thesis."

"So what bumper stickers do you have on your car," she asked again.

"I don't have any," he embarrassingly replied.

"You mean you have nothing to say about where you stand on any of the major issues we face today?" There was a tone of disgust in her question.

The truth was, he didn't know what the major issues were let alone where he stood on those issues. He had lived in an insulated world where his mom cooked his meals and did his laundry. He had thrived in his embryonic sack of his own home life.

"Well, I am against the war in Vietnam."

"Today, everyone is against the war in Vietnam. It is not 1965 anymore," she countered.

"I think Tibet should be free," he said somewhat proudly—although he still wasn't sure what or who was keeping Tibet from actually being free.

She nodded, kind of impressed that he was aware of the fact that China was oppressively occupying Tibet, a small country that was located between China and India.

It was a little after 7 p.m. and the multi-purpose room was now close to full and most of the floor space was occupied with people, blankets and sleeping bags. The lights dimmed and the 16mm projector on the right came to life, beaming a blinding white light on the screen, before the first film appeared. Then, slightly out of focus at first, from Paramount Pictures, was the 1932 release of "Horse Feathers" starring those zany Marx Brothers. It was a comedy that spoofed college life at

Huxley University and revolved around the football team. It took a while for the kids to settle down. Most were still up and down getting sodas and popcorn or moving about and talking with friends.

The Marx Brother's film ended a little after 8 p.m. being only sixty-eight minutes long and a little shorter in length than the rest of the features. Anthony got a kick out of watching Natalie laugh at the antics of Harpo Marx on the screen.

The second movie was, "Paint Your Wagon." It was a good choice for the students. It had been released a few years earlier, in 1969. It was a musical western with some bawdy themes in it. Nothing graphic was on the screen, but it was a bit tantalizing. It ran for a little over two and a half hours. By the last half hour, some students were starting to fall asleep. Others were making out heavily in the darkness and under their blankets. Anthony and Natalie were in the later group. The back wall provided a bit of privacy since everyone was arranged on the floor so that they faced the screen. The yellow comforter was thrown over the two of them and their warm bodies were intertwined together as they let their passion almost reach a boiling point. But there were limits as to what two people could do on the floor of the multi-purpose room in the Forest Fern Complex.

By the end of the third feature at about 1:25 a.m., most people were asleep on the floor, or had gone back to their rooms. A few highly caffeinated people were still enjoying, "The Maltese Falcon" and looking forward to the next film, "The King and I."

Anthony and Natalie had breathlessly fallen asleep in each other's arms, and under the blanket. For the most part, it was pretty innocent; but it would certainly make both of their mothers very uncomfortable. But then again, that's what college was all about.

After Yul Brenner convinces Deborah Kerr to stay in Bangkok, the cafeteria staff cleared the sodas and popcorn from the snack table and started putting out donuts to go along with the two giant stainless steel coffee urns, one with coffee and one with hot chocolate. More and more students were heading back to their rooms.

Only about half of the original crowd was still on hand to watch Roy Rogers and Mary Hart in, "Shine on Harvest Moon" and most of them were asleep. About an hour later the movie ended. The cowboy ends up with the girl. The lights came on in the multi-purpose room and the sleepy movie goers all stood up and stretched their backs, sore from trying to sleep on the floor. Natalie rolled over and opened her eyes. Sitting up and looking about somewhat confused, she shook Anthony to wake him. They both looked at each other then slowly got to their feet. Some students grabbed a donut and coffee or hot chocolate on their way out the door. Most just trudged up the hill in the early morning light, some wrapping their blankets around themselves against the chill in the air.

Anthony, still bleary-eyed, carried the comforter as he walked Natalie back up to the dorm. At her door, he handed her the comforter. Her hair was all messed up and her make-up was mostly gone, but he thought she still looked great. She murmured something inaudible to him. He nodded, kissed her and went back to his room to get some badly needed sleep. It was a good first date.

CHAPTER 24
Looking Southwest

<u>April 1975</u>

Everyone had been at school since September and they had gone through the chill of the long winter months. In spring, the days start getting longer, the temperature starts warming up, and like bears stirring awake from hibernating, they were ready to get out and get into some mischief.

One afternoon, Anthony was passing Tyrone and Dylan's room on his way back from class. He looked in and they were filling a large plastic trashcan with water. Randall was also in the room giving advice to them and Flynn was there helping. The hose was stretched from the spigot behind the water fountain, down the hall a short way, and into their room. The plastic trashcan was the size of an oil drum.

"What the heck is going on?" Anthony asked. They said that Igor walked back from class each afternoon on the service road just below their dorm room. "Well, I have to watch this." Anthony said. Sure enough, just as the can was filled, here comes Igor wearing his trademark bib overalls with oil stains on them. Anthony had doubts that they could hit him with the water from that height and was also afraid that if the can fell too, it would kill Igor. As Anthony watched, it took four of them to lift the water-filled can and get it to the edge of the window. Then they tipped it over and fifty-five gallons of water cascaded down three stories. Although there were also other people on the road, it was a direct hit on Igor with no collateral damage. Dylan and Tyrone followed Randall as they all sprinted back to his room to hide. Flynn ducked out, ran as fast as his hiking boots could carry him and made it safely back to his room. Anthony ran back to his place and closed the door. All of them locked their doors. No one came out of their rooms for like two or three days. Igor, dripping wet, came up to the third-floor yelling, pounding on doors, screaming and vowing to emasculate all of them with his chain saw. He was furious.

Later on, Flynn summed it up perfectly, "Payback's a bitch."

Although Anthony was doing fairly well in school and he was enjoying his relationship with Natalie, he was starting to have doubts about spending all four years of college behind the "Redwood Curtain," as some people called it. He knew that many of his friends were already attending Southwestern State University and he thought it might be cool to reunite with them. There were other universities in the state college system, but at this time, he had enough adventures and wanted to be somewhere familiar, and closer to home.

And it didn't help when he'd occasionally pass Mary Sue in the hallway or on campus. That only reignited his feeling of looking south toward home. Still, he had put it off for several weeks now and finally decided he had to look into it further. He stopped by the Admissions Office on Wednesday afternoon after his Archery class. He sat on a bench outside an admissions counselor's office, waiting for her to finish with another student. There were three other counselors' offices in that hallway and all of them were meeting with students and had more students sitting on benches in the hallway waiting to see them.

They can't all be wanting to transfer, he told himself. Then the words of the speaker at the orientation echoed in his head. "Sequoia State University is a great place, but it's not for everybody." *Maybe they are all transferring*, he thought. *They couldn't have all dated Mary Sue*, he chuckled at his own joke.

"Anthony, come in and have a seat," the counselor said as she walked a young female student out of her office. Anthony walked in and sat at one of the two chairs facing her desk. There were some diplomas and certificates on her wall. A sofa was along the wall to the right. Some framed photos of kids and vacations were on the bookshelf to the left. The counselor sat down on the sofa and Anthony adjusted his chair to face her instead of the vacant desk. It was a disarming move to make the counselee feel more comfortable. *She knows her stuff,* Anthony thought to himself.

"What can we do for you today," she asked, inferring that whatever it was, it was going to be a team effort. That was comforting. *She is good.*

"Uh, well, I am thinking of transferring, maybe to Southwestern State near my home. I was wondering how to go about that?"

"I see. Southwestern is an excellent school. Probably we, and Southwestern are the two most popular state schools in California. Transferring is not difficult. There are just some deadlines to keep in mind."

Sounds easy so far, Anthony thought.

"Tell me though, before we go on, why are you thinking of transferring. We like to be aware of the reasons why people leave us," she asked digging deeper.

"Probably the usual. Closer to home, family, friends."

"Have you made any friends up here so far this school year?" she asked probing deeper.

"Oh, yes. I live in the dorms, and everybody there is very nice. My roommate is a great guy. The LGA's do a great job," he said praising all.

"Have you lost any friends up here so far this school year?" she asked further. *Oh, she's good. She's very good.*

Anthony paused a second and then asked, "Why do you ask that?"

"It's just that we find one of the many reasons people transfer from school can be social issues. The dorms are a pretty compressed, isolated yet very dynamic social environment. Relationships, like storm clouds can form quickly with a lot of energy and then dissipate just as quickly. In the meantime, they can cause a lot of damage. We talk to our LGA's constantly about being supportive and being extra aware of the connections students are making in the dorms."

Anthony wondered if Jeff, the LGA, had been keeping a secret dossier on him and the counselor had it on her desk right now. The old saying, "Just because you're paranoid, doesn't mean they are not after you," went through his mind.

"Well, there was one little speed bump we hit along the way, but that's over and certainly not the reason for my wanting to transfer," he assured her.

"That's fine then. Why don't you write down your name and dorm address and I will call Southwestern in the morning and have them mail you a transfer packet." She stood up indicating the meeting was over. She shook his hand and he left feeling good about taking the first step. He knew his parents would be happy to have him home again.

In the hallway, he made a mental note to explain all this to Natalie as soon as the time was right. Then it sort of slipped his mind.

CHAPTER 25
Natalie

Natalie woke up Wednesday morning with a stuffy nose and was sneezing and coughing. Every few minutes she was blowing her nose—to the point that Lena, who loved her like a sister, was starting to get annoyed because she had kept her up all night. Natalie skipped that morning's classes and stayed in bed resting.

At 11 a.m., Anthony walked out of his Personnel Management class and cruised across campus. The weather was gloomy that morning and the cloud cover still blocked out the sun. As Anthony walked past the student union building, he noticed a lot of people standing around watching television in the student lounge. They had somber looks on their faces, so he ducked in to see what was happening.

ABC News had interrupted its regular broadcast for a special news bulletin about the fall of Saigon in Vietnam. There was a lot of movement by the camera as it panned from some gate that people were pressed up against to a tall building where people were climbing to the roof. A helicopter had approached and landed on the rooftop and people were clamoring to get onboard.

They cut away to another scene aboard an aircraft carrier, its flight deck covered with people. Sailors were pushing a perfectly good helicopter over the side of the ship and into the ocean to make room for more evacuees. In both scenes, one could feel the terror and chaos of what was happening. Mothers holding children, old people afraid and confused, people dropping their luggage and simply running for their lives.

The announcer said the Vietnam War was over. We had lost. The announcer was stunned. The students gathered around the television were stunned. Anthony, who had not really followed the news leading up to all of this, could still sense the gravity of the situation. He felt badly as he watched the anguish in the faces of the people and knowing this was live TV. It was happening right now. Again, Anthony realized he had to become more informed of issues and more supportive of just causes.

He left the student union and walked toward his dorm. He was hit by the contrast between what he had seen on TV and the idyllic atmosphere of a college campus—people walking and talking in small groups; a person sitting on a bench, reading a book; two people playing with a Frisbee on the grass. He felt fortunate to be in such an idyllic place but wondered if it somehow insulated him from what was happening in the rest of the world. Still, since he had left the sheltered life of home to come up to Sequoia State, he had been protectively exposed to some of the important issues of the day—something that might not have happened if he had never left Orange County.

Anthony bounded up the stairs and at the top, turned right into the girls' hallway. He had not seen Natalie at breakfast in the dining hall, so he thought he would stop by her room. When he walked in, she was in bed with the covers up to her chin and looked terrible.

"What happened to you?" he exclaimed.

"I'm thick," she answered with a stuffed-up nose.

"Is there anything I can do to make you feel better?"

"Just leave me alone. Lena is taking good care of me."

Anthony glanced over at Lena, who was studying at her desk. She looked at Anthony and just rolled her eyes.

Anthony sat on the floor and leaned up against Natalie's bed and quietly went over his notes from class. In the silence, with Lena studying and Natalie falling sleeping, Anthony realized that with Natalie, he didn't have to be talking all the time. He was comfortable with her, even in silence. This was an aspect of a relationship he had not before experienced.

At about 12:30 p.m., Anthony was getting hungry for lunch. He asked if either of the girls wanted him to bring back something for them to eat, to which they declined. He went to the dining hall and picked out an entre. Buzz was nowhere to be seen, so he must have had the day off. After lunch, Anthony walked past the salad bar and grabbed two small packages of saltine crackers and put them in his jacket pocket.

Walking out of the dining hall, he ran smack into Mary Sue.

"Hey, I've been wanting to talk to you," she said as if she might have wanted to talk about the weather or some other trivial thing.

"About what?" Anthony asked most surprised. They hadn't spoken since that day outside the bookstore.

"About what happened between us."

Anthony looked up and down the hallway outside the dining hall. It seemed like an inappropriate place for a sensitive conversation.

"I don't really want to talk about it," he stated.

"I think we need to. I think the time is right since you are now involved again," apparently referring to Natalie. Her last sentence almost had a hint of an accusation in it.

"You're commenting on my relationship with someone else?" he asked incredulously. He was thinking, *That is like the pot calling the kettle black.*

"I didn't mean that at all!" she said with anger growing in her voice.

Other people in the hallway were starting to look at the pair as their confrontation was becoming more heated. Anthony was becoming more and more uncomfortable with the situation.

"Listen, what's done is done. I'm okay with it. I have moved on. Thank you for caring enough to want to explain, but I'd rather you didn't. Just go."

Mary Sue made an abrupt about face and stormed off in the opposite direction. She had the best of intentions, and it blew up in her face.

Anthony turned around and walked away, embarrassed by the small crowd of gawkers who had gathered listening to the two of them. He started walking up the path to the dorms and then he remembered his plan. He switched paths and walked over to the bookstore.

Inside, he walked to the bookstore's small grocery aisle. They carried a few cans of chili, bags of chips, and three kinds of donuts—powdered sugar, crumb, and paraffin wax chocolate. Below the cans of chili were a few cans of chicken soup. Anthony grabbed one of the cans and went to the register and paid for it.

Running back up to his room, he grabbed a red felt pen from his desk and drew a heart and the words, "Get Well," on the lid of the can. He walked out of his room and turned up the girls' hallway. By sheer chance, coming from the opposite direction was Mary Sue. When she saw Anthony at the other end of the hallway, she glared at him. They both continued walking; she, toward her room; he, toward Natalie's room. They looked like two cowboy gunfighters about to have it out on Main Street. When they were still twenty feet apart, she walked into the open door of her room and slammed it so hard it sounded like a gunshot. Anthony considered feigning that he had been shot and falling to the ground playing dead but decided against it. Everyone else in the hallway jumped at the sound.

Anthony walked into Natalie's room. Lena was not there, but Natalie sat up in bed and asked in a startled voice, "What in the hell was that?"

"Just another disgruntled postal worker I suppose," he said. She didn't get his humor. He handed her the chicken soup with the lid pointed towards her so she could read the inscription. You would have thought he had given her a dozen red roses. She was so touched.

"You are so sweet," she said as she flopped back on the bed. "When I don't feel like puking, I will enjoy having it."

So romantic, Anthony thought to himself.

———————

That night, there was a knock at Anthony and Don's door. Flynn was going down the hallway, recruiting people to go down to the California Highway Patrol Office to steal the big, golden bear statue that sat out in front of the station. Flynn had on a ski mask covering his entire face except for the mouth and eyeholes. Randall had on a camouflage jacket. He looked like he was going duck hunting. Tyrone and Dylan were dressed all in black. The six of them jumped in Flynn's Jeep and drove down the hill to the CHP office near Highway 101. Dylan jumped out and scouted the area. There was a one-story cinderblock building with a big window in the front of it. Through the window, you could see the radio dispatcher at his desk. Dylan came back to the Jeep that was parked about a half a block away in a field and reported what he saw. Besides the dispatcher, there was no one else in the area. Flynn drove the Jeep with its lights off to the edge of the gravel parking lot in front of the station. Next to the flagpole was the bear statue. The six of them silently approached the statue. With three of them on one side and three on the other, they tried to lift it to gauge if they could carry it. It was heavy and looked like it would barely fit in the back of the Jeep. Anthony pictured all of them getting arrested and kicked out of school. The adrenalin was definitely pumping. They lifted the statue and got it almost all the way to the Jeep, when a voice came over the P.A. system in the parking lot. The dispatcher, who was watching them from behind the big window said, "Don't drop it." At that point, Anthony realized they weren't committing a crime. It turns out the bear was actually made by a Sequoia State art student several years ago and then it was given to the CHP. Each year, some students steal the bear, but always return it. It looked funny as they drove off into the night with this huge bear's butt sticking out of the back of the Jeep, while all of them hung on for dear life. Anthony thought to himself, *This is GREAT!*

They used the bear statue for the centerpiece of a party that weekend in the dorm lounge area. Later the next week, the vile, evil members of rival dorm stole the bear. Shocked by this act of aggression, they considered an all-out assault, a nuclear attack, or a commando raid to regain possession of the coveted golden bear. Then Vance, the dorm wise-man with a much cooler head reminded them that whoever ended up with the bear had to bring it back down the hill and return it to the

CHP. Impressed by the guru's wisdom, they let the rival dorm's transgression pass without retribution.

The bear was returned to the CHP office the following week without any loss of life.

CHAPTER 26
Seeking Protection

In the meantime, Anthony and Natalie's relationship was getting more serious in a physical kind of way. Anthony didn't know if or when "something" might happen, but he wanted to be prepared. He decided it would be best if he had some, "protection." Never having been in a totally physical relationship before, he did not know where to purchase the prior mentioned product—or say three-pack of the product. He figured, being on a college campus, they must be available somewhere. However, he didn't want to raise any suspicion, so he didn't ask anyone in the dorms how to get them.

A few days later, when his classes were over for the day, he walked into town. He would try the local drugstore. Anthony walked in and started walking up and down the aisles. He could not find them anywhere. He thought for sure the drugstore would carry something like that. Finally, he found a guy stocking bandages and other first aid items on the shelf in the middle of the store. As Anthony walked up to him, an old lady was coming down the aisle the other way. Anthony paused slightly, then continued walking past the guy stocking shelves, not wanting the old lady to hear his question. He walked on to the next aisle and pretended to look at greeting cards. After a moment, he returned to the aisle with the stock clerk. He looked up and down the aisle. No one was else was present. It was just a man-to-man question, yet Anthony was hesitant. Finally, he just blurted it out.

"Where do you have rubbers?" he asked.

"You mean condoms?" the stock guy asked him.

"Uh, yes." Anthony felt bad he hadn't known the correct terminology.

"You gotta ask the pharmacist. They keep them behind the counter," he replied.

Anthony walked to the back of the store to the pharmacy section. He gave a sigh of relief, as there were no customers dropping off or picking up any prescriptions. He gathered up his confidence since he was now aware of the correct terminology. He walked up to the counter and rang the bell to summon the pharmacist from the back. After a moment, the pharmacist came to the counter. Correction, the female pharmacist came to the counter, an attractive, 40-something year old, female pharmacist.

"Can I help you?" she asked politely.

For a moment, Anthony was stunned. He just stared at her in disbelief. Gathering every fiber of bravery that he could, he reminded himself that this was the 1970s, not the 1950s.

"I'd like a pack of condoms," he said in a hushed tone. Then, the questions started.

"Three-pack or twelve-pack?"

"Vibra-ribbed or regular?"

"Lubricated or plain?"

"Rainbow colors or reservoir-tip?"

YOU'VE GOT TO BE KIDDING ME! Anthony thought to himself as he answered each question, not even sure what she was asking or what his answers meant. Finally, she reached under the counter and put a small blue box in a white pharmacy bag and folded down the top.

Thank God, Anthony thought to himself. It was almost over.

"Let me see. I forget the price on these." Then she reached for the microphone to the store loudspeaker system. "Price check in Pharmacy," echoed throughout the store.

Anthony almost had a heart attack.

"What is it," the guy at the front cash register yelled back to her.

"Here," Anthony stammered. "Please take the five-dollar bill and we'll call it even."

"Condoms," she answered over the loudspeaker again.

"What kind?" he yelled back to her.

"Please, please don't answer him. Here, I'll give you ten dollars," which was all the money he had on him at the moment. He felt sure he was in a Woody Allen movie where everything that could go wrong, did go wrong—and it wasn't over yet.

"Oh, I'm sure it is not that much," the pharmacist said sweetly. Again, to the microphone she answered, "Three-pack, Vibra-ribbed, plain, reservoir-tip."

Anthony was sure he was going to pass out from so much blood rushing to his completely crimson, blushing face.

"A buck seventy-five," came the final answer.

"See, it wasn't nearly as expensive as you thought dear," the pharmacist said sweetly as she rang up the sale on the cash register.

Anthony paid, picked up his change and the little white bag and walked to the front of the store trying hard not to make eye contact with anyone, especially the little old lady.

Outside the store, he paused to gather his composure. He hoped that if they did do "it," they wouldn't do it more than three times because he was sure he couldn't go through all this again.

———————

The next day before his class started, Anthony stopped by Natalie's room to check on her. He was surprised to see that she was up and around and getting ready to go to class—certainly a fast recovery. On the other hand, Lena was now under her covers, blowing her nose and sneezing, with the same cold that Natalie had the day before.

Anthony then walked Natalie to her lecture hall before heading to his class. They talked casually and were enjoying the crisp-but-clear spring weather. She said that she would stop by his room on her way back from class in an hour or so. That was good for Anthony, because he knew that Don would be in counseling for a few hours.

In the springtime, it was difficult to concentrate on what the professors were saying in class. It was difficult to keep ones mind from wandering to thoughts of all kinds of things...

"That's all for today. Please make sure you've read Chapter 16 by our next class meeting." And with that, class was over. Anthony bolted out the door and took the stairs two at a time. Turning left into his hallway, he unlocked his door and went inside. He left the door open and tossed his textbook on his desk, which also had, yellow tablets, mail, notecards and various other items scattered about on it. He grabbed a candy bar from the bookshelf, opened it, sat down and started to read Chapter 16.

Natalie had gotten out of class and went back to her room to check on Lena and to change clothes. Lena was asleep, so Natalie went to her closet and changed what she was wearing. She put on a heavy jacket from her closet and quietly left her room so Lena could continue to get some rest.

Down the hall, she turned into the boys' hallway and walked into Anthony's room. He was sitting at his desk with his back to the door. Quietly, she closed the door and removed the heavy coat. Underneath, she was wearing the school uniform, bib overalls...and nothing else. Both straps were up and snapped, but no shirt underneath it. In fact, no nothing underneath it except her firm, curvaceous body. She walked up quietly behind Anthony and bending slightly, pressed herself against his shoulders and the back of his neck. She moved her head to the right side of Anthony's head, kissing him on the neck, and then playfully bit his ear. Anthony turned and his eyes almost popped out of his head. He turned his chair ninety degrees from his desk, and she straddled him, as they both kissed passionately. He lowered his head and kissed her throat. She raised her head sensually, and one of the straps slid off her bare shoulder. Enjoying the sensation, she then turned her head towards the desk to expose more of the soft, sensitive skin of her neck. Anthony was calculating his next move, when...

"WHAT THE HELL IS THIS?" she screamed. She held a piece of mail from his desk in her hands. It was a transfer application from Southwestern State University.

Dear Anthony:

Thank you for your request for information on how to transfer to Southwestern State University. Please find the enclosed transfer application and all necessary supporting documents...

"Let me explain," Anthony said completely stunned at how quickly things had gone from great to horrible. "I was only thinking about it. I was going to tell you."

"Well, you hadn't gotten around to it yet. My god, and I was going to..." she didn't finish her sentence. Anthony thought her screaming sounded like Major Houlihan on M*A*S*H. She got up, threw her jacket on over her bare shoulders and stormed out of the room.

Anthony exhaled, considered taking a cold shower, then turned towards his desk and reread the letter from Southwestern.

CHAPTER 27
Meeting Him

Rumors were swirling around the third floor dorm that Mary Sue's boyfriend was again coming down to school for a visit. He had been to school over a weekend in November, but this would be his first visit in his new role as fiancé.

Although this didn't bother Anthony since he had only spoken to Mary Sue once since January, he was still kind of curious about taking a look at ol' Jim.

The first thing Anthony had to do however was find Natalie and explain the letter she had read yesterday in his room. He went to her room, but she wasn't there—just Lena who was studying. When he asked her about Natalie, she aloofly told him that she didn't know where Natalie was at the moment, nor when she might return. Apparently, she also took umbrage with the fact that Anthony planned to slink out of town under the cover of darkness without telling anyone about it. Anthony rolled his eyes and walked down the hall, not sure where Natalie might be.

Later that afternoon on Friday, he looked out of the window in his dorm room and saw Natalie walking back from class toward the dorm. He raced out of his room, down the hall, and down the steps and met her just as she was coming in the door to the stairway.

"Hey, we've got to talk," he said reaching for her hand.

She jerked her hand away from his, but didn't turn away from him, apparently wanting to hear what he had to say.

As his voice echoed a bit in the stairwell, he started, "I was going to tell you, but I didn't know exactly what I was going to say because I am still not sure what I am going to do. I haven't even told Don about it yet. I had thought that I might transfer to Southwestern because I kind of missed home and I am not sure I wanted to stay at Sequoia State for all four years. I was just looking into it. In fact, you're the biggest reason I have for staying at Sequoia. I am pretty certain I will stay, and I should have told you about it. I am sorry." He paused as several people came down the stairs and out the door.

"You should have told me," she said crossly. "I thought I meant something to you."

"You do. And again, I am sorry," he said penitently. She started up the stairs as he stood on the ground floor looking up at her. "Can I see you tonight?" he asked cautiously.

"If you're lucky," she said defiantly as she looked down on him from over the railing. He thought he could detect a subtle smile that she was trying hide from him. *Again, the cat playing with the mouse,* he thought.

He was still leaning toward leaving for Southwestern State, but he didn't want to do anything to mess things up with Natalie as long as he was at Sequoia State.

The girls on third floor were giddy with excitement to see Jim again, especially now since he and Mary Sue were engaged. He was to arrive Friday night and stay until Sunday morning. He had to get back to feed the hogs or milk the cows or do whatever you do to apple trees.

As much as Anthony was over Mary Sue, he was building up a sincere dislike for this guy. He was sure he must be a jerk, in fact he kind of hoped that was the case. That is what Mary deserved—a lifetime spent married to jerk-face. Anthony wondered how tough he was, how big he was, how smart he was. These things festered in Anthony until there was a simmering rage boiling over in him.

Friday after dinner in the dining hall, Anthony walked over to Natalie's room and asked her if she wanted to go to the movies in town. He certainly didn't want to be around when Jim the "Wonder Stud" showed up...not that he cared.

Natalie agreed and got her stuff and headed downstairs. They crossed the bridge over Highway 101 and strolled down the street to the theatre near the town square. They bought tickets for the seven o'clock showing of "The Sting" and went in and sat near the back of the theatre.

"So, what do you think of Mary Sue's fiancé coming up to visit her," she asked pointedly.

"I really hadn't given it much thought," he lied.

She left it at that and didn't ask any more questions. She did rest her hand on his leg during the movie, a subtle, but provocative move on her part. *Cat and mouse*, Anthony thought again. He had trouble concentrating on the complicated and intertwining plot of the movie while she had her hand on his thigh.

"Why did they shoot her?" Natalie whispered during the movie.

"She was the assassin," he whispered back.

"I thought the other guy was the assassin," the whispering continued.

"He's the guy Gondorff hired to protect Hooker," he again whispered back.

"Hooker as in the prostitute, or Johnny Hooker? I am so confused," she went on again.

Someone a few rows in front of them turned around and sternly said, "Shhhhhh!" and gave them a dirty look. Natalie stuck her tongue out at the person.

"Johnny Hooker," Anthony whispered hoping that was the last of the questions.

When the movie ended, most of the people in the theatre clapped because as the movie was about tricking someone, it was also about tricking the audience. On the way back to campus, Natalie asked a million questions about the movie and why this happened or that happened. Being that the movie got out a little after 9 p.m., and Anthony knew that Don was studying in their room that night, and "Prince Charming" Jim had probably arrived already, Anthony had another thought.

The library was open until 10 p.m. on Friday nights. Anthony was holding hands with Natalie and guided her past the service road that led up to the dorm and took a path that lead to the library. Natalie, not sure what was going on, followed along.

"I need to get a book for class," he lied again for the second time tonight as they entered the library.

"Sure," she said.

"I think it is on the fourth floor," he said stepping into the elevator and pressing the number four button.

The doors to the elevator closed and lifted them up to the top floor of the library. When the doors opened, they saw that there was practically no one the fourth floor. Anthony, still holding Natalie's hand, led her around to the far side of the bookshelves.

Putting two and two together in her head she asked, "Is Don studying in your room tonight?" Anthony nodded and pulled her close to him as he sat on the edge of a small study table. They embraced and the fiery passion of two young lovers started to ignite. They paused for a minute as someone walked by the far end of the bookshelves. They heard the elevator door glide open for a moment and then shut. Knowing that they were probably the only ones on the fourth floor now, Natalie pulled Anthony over to a couch along the wall. As they sat down together, Natalie laid back and pulled Anthony on top of her. In the torrid moment, Anthony's hands were all over her and she was moaning with pleasure.

"The library will be closing in five minutes," came an announcement over the library speaker system. Both of them sat up quickly, still breathing hard. They looked at each other with hungry eyes. They wanted each other so badly, but realized it wasn't going to happen tonight. Anthony was frustrated, but at least it wasn't like last time when Natalie had left his room in a rage over the letter. They stood up, straightened their clothes, and got on the elevator. When the elevator door closed, Natalie turned toward Anthony and pressed him against the side wall, again kissing him passionately. Just as the door opened on the ground floor, she stopped and they walked out casually as if nothing had happened.

When they got to the top of the stairs in the dorms, he pulled her close this time and kissed her passionately again.

"It sounds like a good book you were looking for. I can't wait to read the ending," she said coyly.

She is so good at double-entendres, thought Anthony. He smiled and kissed her again before they went down their respective hallways to their rooms.

Anthony walked in as Don was putting one book away and opening another. It had been a long night for him and was going to get longer before it was over. Don nodded at him and continued working. Anthony got into bed and turned away from the light on Don's desk. He was happy that Natalie had forgiven him and things were looking good for both of them and their relationship.

———————

    Saturday morning, Don and Anthony headed down the path for an early breakfast in the dining hall. Unbeknownst to them, Mary Sue and Jim were also walking down to eat because they wanted to get an early start on some local sightseeing.

    Anthony saw the couple coming out of the doorway at the far end of their dorm. Don was oblivious for the moment, still bleary-eyed from a long night of studying. Anthony was surprised that Jim was a handsome looking guy, with an athletic build. He had a stylish moustache that was well trimmed. He wore and denim jacket with a wooly collar and Lee jeans of course. He also had on a pair of cowboy boots. He certainly looked the part, Anthony thought.

    The happy couple was slightly ahead of Don and Anthony as they entered the dining hall. They put their stuff down at a table near the large windows that overlooked the forest. Don and Anthony headed into the cafeteria line and were soon joined by Jim. Mary Sue was just having some coffee, which she got at the coffee station just outside the cafeteria entrance.

    When Anthony saw Jim in line right next to him, he sort of sneered at him. Jim wasn't even looking at Anthony as he was checking out the day's faire for breakfast. Don had no idea who the guy behind Anthony was, and Mary Sue hadn't noticed Don and Anthony walking in behind them. Anthony was the only one who was aware of the awkward moment created by their serendipitous crossing of paths.

    "Man, I could eat the whole left side of the menu, I'm so hungry," Jim said to Don and Anthony, referring to the press-on letter board with today's offerings listed. Don laughed at the joke. "You guys look like you enjoy a good meal. What's good here?" he asked in a friendly manner.

"Hey, you gotta try the three-egg omelet that Buzz cooks up. Can't be beat!" Don was really enjoying chatting with this guy who he had never met before.

When Buzz came out of the back, Don said, "Buzz, can you make my friend one of your special three-egg omelets?"

"Sure thing!" Buzz replied, proud to have a reputation as a great omelet cook.

Anthony was looking at the whole scene and rolling his eyes and trying to give Don the "high sign" without Jim seeing him. He was trying to alert Don as to the fact that this is not just some guy he was chatting with. It was Mary Sue's fiancé! Don had no clue.

When Buzz proudly served Jim the now famous omelet, he said, "Thanks Buzz and thanks you guys. It looks great. I appreciate you pointing me in the right direction."

I'd like to point you in the right direction, right over a cliff! Anthony was thinking to himself.

Don replied, "Sure thing buddy. Any time." Even Buzz looked on at Jim with admiration.

Anthony was beside himself. After he and Don got their meals, they headed into the dining area and Anthony chose a table as far away as possible from the happy couple.

"Are you freakin' crazy?" Anthony admonished Don in a low but forceful voice.

"What are you talking about?" Don asked as if he had no idea what Anthony meant.

"Do you know who your 'omelet buddy' was back there? It was JIM!" That still didn't register with Don. "As in Jim, Mary Sue's fiancé!"

"No way," Don replied looking around to try to see where the guy was sitting.

The normally loyal-as-a-canine Don defended himself, "Well, he seems like a nice guy, didn't he?"

He was rather friendly, and cool, and handsome, Anthony thought to himself. The kind of guy you'd want on your team; or more accurately, you'd want to be on HIS team.

"That doesn't matter," Anthony blurted out, he said both to Don and himself. "He's Mary Sue's fiancé, and if I want to hate him, I will."

"Don't be such a dick-head," Don said to Anthony. "I thought you were over Mary Sue. He seems like a nice guy. Don't be like an old lady in a trailer park."

Anthony didn't quite know what that meant, but figured it wasn't good. And it was hard not to like the guy. He seemed very down-to-earth, the real deal. Anthony could tell you could trust him, that his word was his bond.

After finishing their breakfast, Don and Anthony left the dining hall. Don was still shaking his head, and Anthony was still not sure what to think of Jim. As they walked past the happy couple, who were still eating, Mary Sue looked up and saw Don and Anthony for the first time that morning and was somewhat startled, but didn't say anything to anyone.

Sunday morning, Jim left for Hilland and things returned to normal. Anthony hoped that Don would do some more studying in the library this week. So did Natalie.

CHAPTER 28
A Broken Heart

<u>May 1975</u>

In late May, at 4:15 p.m. in the afternoon, Anthony was working at his desk on a final project for his Personnel Management class. Don was in the library working on a project for his Structural Engineering class. Suddenly, Lena came running to the open door and leaned in breathlessly.

"Come quick, Anthony! Natalie just got a phone call from home and she's really upset."

Anthony couldn't comprehend what the crisis might be. It seemed that it was worse than any dorm drama. He pushed away from his desk, flipping his pencil on top of the yellow tablet he was using for his rough draft and sprinted out the door following Lena to their room. When he walked into the room, Natalie was sitting on the bed, her eyes were red and she was still crying. Lena sat down next to her and hugged her and she started crying also. Anthony sat on the other side of Natalie and put his arms around the both of them as best he could. A death in the family was all he could think that it might be.

"Natalie, what's the matter? What happened?" he asked.

"My dad," and she started to cry again.

He looked at Lena and she mouthed quietly, "I think he had a heart attack." Anthony nodded and looked at Natalie.

"Mom found him on the floor in the garage. She didn't know how long he had been out there. He had been working on fixing a chair for her. She called the ambulance and they took him to the hospital. Everyone is there now...except me!"

"Don't worry," he said. "We'll get you home." He started to pull away, but she grabbed his arm and pulled him close and started crying again.

He looked at Lena and said, "You take care of her and help her pack some things. I'll go to the campus travel office and explain the situation. We'll try to get her out on the next flight to Ventura Regional Airport. Then we'll figure out how to get her to the airport. I think Don might be able to drive us." Lena nodded and Anthony pulled away from Natalie.

At the travel office, Anthony explained what had happened and the lady phoned someone, then went to a drawer and pulled out a blank airline ticket and wrote the information on it. The ticket cost $48. A bit more than usual since it was requested at the last minute and since it was to a regional airport. It was a 6:30 p.m. flight that landed in Ventura at 7:10 p.m. that night. Anthony paid cash from his money envelope that he took from the desk in his room. He sprinted across campus, hoping Don would be back in the room after studying in the library. Anthony took the stairs two at a time, passing people coming down, but not bothering to acknowledge anyone. At the top landing he turned left into his hallway and then through the open door of his room. Don was putting books back on his wall-mounted bookshelf and turned towards him.

"Natalie's dad had a heart attack and she is flying home tonight. Can you give us a ride to the airport? We leave in an hour and a half," Anthony blurted out the facts.

Don was stunned but reacted quickly. "Absolutely. Let me go put gas in the beast and I will pull up next to the dorms at 5:30 sharp."

Anthony returned to the girls' room and helped Natalie pack. She only took one suitcase, leaving most everything else. She wasn't sure how long she would be gone. Then Natalie said she was going to get cleaned up and shower before leaving for the airport. Anthony used the time run down to the dining hall for a quick bite to eat. He put an apple in his pocket to give to Natalie to eat on the flight. He knew she probably didn't want dinner but she might get hungry on the flight. Returning to the third floor, Anthony took a quick shower and dressed. It was 5:20 when Anthony closed the door to his room and headed back to the girls' room.

The girls were both sitting next to each other on the bed. Both looked sad. Both had red eyes from crying, but neither one was crying at the moment. One small white suitcase sat on the floor—the sleeve of a blouse partly hanging out one side was evidence of how fast everything was thrown together.

"Can I come to the airport too?" Lena asked reluctantly.

"Sure, you can. There should be room if this is the only luggage we have. We better go. Don will be waiting." The two girls stood up as Anthony grabbed the suitcase. They followed him down the stairs and out the door. On the service road next to the dorm, Don had just pulled up and the car was still running. Anthony popped the trunk and threw in the suitcase. Lena let Anthony and Natalie slide into the back seat, then hopped in the front passenger seat and closed the door. Don gunned the engine then the car whipped a U-turn and headed down the street towards the on-ramp to Highway 101 north.

The four of them traveled in silence most of the way. Lena had turned around in her seat and was letting her fingers intertwine with Natalie's fingers in a silent show of support as they drove. They wheeled into the gravel parking lot and Don parked in a space not too far from the log terminal, such as it was. Anthony retrieved the suitcase and together they walked into the terminal. Natalie checked in and got her boarding pass. They sat down on fiberglass chairs that looked like they belonged in Disney's Tomorrowland in 1955 rather than in a log building in the Pacific Northwest in 1975. Anthony felt something in his pocket and remembered the apple. He gave it to Natalie, and he could see the practical and sentimental appreciation in her eyes. Soon they called to board the flight. The four of them walked out of the log building to the forty-two inch tall chain link fence. They were boarding through Gate 2.

Natalie hugged Don and thanked him for the ride. Then she turned to Lena who was now gushing tears. They hugged tight a long time. "You are the sister I never had," Natalie told Lena.

"I know. And you are the same to me," Lena replied. They stepped apart, looked at each other and started laughing through their tears.

Finally, Natalie turned to Anthony. They hugged warmly. "Thanks for everything," she said.

"Don't worry. Let me know how you are doing and how things are going with your dad," Anthony replied.

She hugged him close again and kissed him gently one last time. She let go, picked up her suitcase and walked through Gate 2 and across the concrete, climbed the roll-up stairway, and on to the smallish, Boeing 727. The remaining three stood at the fence looking at the airliner hoping that Natalie could see them even though they could not see through the plane's small, tinted windows at all. After everyone was on board, the tractor pushed the plane out to the taxiway where the twin jet engines roared to life and warmed up for several minutes. Then the plane made the long, slow journey to the far end of the runway. Don, Lena and Anthony were still leaning on the fence as the plane roared down the runway with its bright running lights flashing and lifted slowly and gracefully into the air. The plane easily cleared the trees at the edge of the airport property and slowly gained altitude. The trio stared as it rose towards the sunset over the Pacific Ocean and then banked left and turned southward toward Ventura. The plane got so small in the distance that one could only see the flashing lights until they too faded from view.

CHAPTER 29
School's Almost Out

June 1975

After class on Wednesday, Anthony walked over to the Forest Fern Complex to check his mailbox. He could see something through the little window, so he dug for his key in his pocket and opened the box. It was a letter from Natalie. He hadn't heard from her since she left school a few weeks ago. Lena had talked to her once on the phone and shared with Anthony that things were not going well for her father and that Natalie was very distraught.

Anthony opened the envelope and sat down on a bench opposite the mailboxes. He took out a single, plain sheet of paper and unfolded it. There was a personal check inside the folded letter. As he read her words, he could hear her voice.

> *Dear Anthony,*
>
> *I hope you are well. Things are tough here right now. Dad is doing slightly better, but not much. Mom is beside herself trying to take care of him and do all the things around the house that he used to do. My brothers are taking care of the outside stuff, like keeping the cars in good running order and mowing the lawn and stuff. Mom needs so much help though.*
>
> *I talked to my professors and of the four classes I am taking, one is pass-fail and I already have enough points to pass. The other three professors agreed to let me mail my final projects to them. One class has a final exam, which the professor will mail me and I will return to her.*

With all that is going on at home, I am going to transfer to Bay Shore Community College here in Ventura so I can live at home. They have accepted me for the fall term as a second-year student. I probably won't take a full load. That way, I have more time to help my mom. Not sure what I will do after that.

I am sorry that I left so quickly, but I knew you would understand. You're the best.

Love,
Natalie

He unfolded the check and saw that it was for $48. She had written it to pay him back for the airplane ticket. On the memo line of the check were three small heart-shaped figures.

Sequoia State University is a great place, but it's not for everybody. But nobody could have predicted that Natalie's experience at Sequoia State would end this way.

Anthony sat on the bench for a long time. Fate had dealt Natalie and her family a bad hand. There was not a lot he could do to help. He walked up to Lena's room and asked her if there was anything she needed. Lena was fighting back tears, but said she was helping Natalie on this end by picking up stuff from her professors and mailing things back and forth between them. She said that she had packed all of Natalie's stuff in the room and that one of Natalie's brothers was driving up this weekend to get it. Tears continued to stream down Lena's face. Anthony wasn't sure if the tears were for her friend's tough situation or because her best friend had to leave school. Maybe it was both. Anthony told her to let him know if there was anything he could do to help and she agreed. He gave her a comforting hug.

As Anthony turned to leave her room, he glanced at one of the boxes of Natalie's stuff. On the top of the box was the stuffed teddy bear that he had given her a few months ago. It too looked sad.

The day before everyone had to be out of the dorms, Anthony was in his room packing and also doing some studying for Math 153, the last final of the semester. As he went back and forth between packing and studying, he came to the conclusion that he had accumulated more stuff than he originally started out with. He decided he had to find some boxes for all the extra things he now possessed.

As Anthony was jamming a Sequoia State sweatshirt into one of the over-stuffed suitcases, Randall walked in to say good-bye. Several people who had completed all their finals; like Tyrone Dylan, and Flynn; had already said their good-byes and had moved out of the dorms. Still, most of the people on third floor had not moved out yet.

"Are you all done?" Anthony asked.

"Yep. Final projects and reports are handed in; and all final exams completed. I turned my key into Jeff and my stuff is being picked up by UPS within the hour." Randall had way too much stuff to put in his Alpha Romero.

"How's Keisha?" Anthony wanted to know.

"She's good. We are going to see each other during the summer. She's going to come up to Berkley in July and I will go to L.A. at the beginning of August. Then we'll be up here in September. She's renting a little craftsmen-style bungalow in town with three other girls and I am getting an apartment nearby. We'll see where we spend the most time together."

"Well, be careful and don't get shot this summer," meaning in L.A.

"No worries. My mom doesn't even own a gun," Randall joked as they both laughed at his dark humor.

They gave each other brotherly hugs and Randall left to flag down the UPS man who would be pulling up on the service road behind the dorm very soon.

Don had been working very hard preparing for his Engineering final. He had been spending many hours in the library and the Engineering Lab. Anthony hadn't seen much of him lately and he wasn't sure why.

Leaving his door open in case anyone else was coming over to say good-bye, Anthony went back to work packing and studying. He was reviewing a formula for Population Variance for his Math 153 final, when he heard some noise coming down the hallway.

"Goodbye Mary, goodbye Jim!"

"See you, Mary Sue. Good luck you two!"

"Bye Mary. 'Love you gal!"

"Have a great summer, Mary Sue!"

Apparently, Jim was helping Mary Sue bring the last of her stuff down the hall, down the stairs and to his Ford F-150 pick-up truck parked on the service road, probably next to the UPS truck for which Randall was waiting.

By the sound and volume of the voices, he knew exactly where Mary Sue was in the hallway as she approached his open door. She had her arms full of some clothes and fragile miscellaneous items, one of which was a driftwood and seashell mobile. She followed Jim who was carrying the heavy stuff.

Anthony sat frozen at his desk as he read and reread the formula for Population Variance:

$$\sigma^2 = \Sigma \, (Xi - \upsilon)^2 / N$$

He debated what to do. If she had been alone on her way down the hallway, he definitely would have said good-bye. After all, they had shared a lot about themselves with each other, even though it had been painful at times. But she was now with Jim, her fiancé. He knew that he couldn't say anything that he felt or wanted to say without embarrassing her in front of him. So, he chose to say nothing, and he did not even look that way as she passed by his door. His eyes got slightly watery as he sat in silence, but no real tears. Don would still be pissed.

When Mary Sue, who was following Jim, turned the corner to the boys' hallway, her heart sank when she saw Anthony's open door ahead on the left. She hoped that Don was the only one in the room. As she passed, she glanced in and saw Anthony studying at his desk. She would have liked at least a smile from him, but she too understood the dynamics of the situation. Moving down the hall, Mary Sue continued to say "Good-bye" to other people, but she felt bad as she left "Antonio" behind forever.

Anthony passed his Math 153 final exam later that afternoon. He hadn't seen Don in quite some time, so he went to dinner in the dining hall by himself. There was a limited menu since the dining hall was getting ready to close for the school year the next day. As Anthony ate his dinner in silence, he reflected on his experience up at school. It had been a heck of a time, he thought.

That night, Anthony went to sleep early. Don was still not back, probably still studying in the library or the Engineering Lab. Most of Anthony's stuff was packed. He still needed to get the bathroom stuff out of his locker in the restroom. Don had some of his stuff in boxes but still had a lot more to pack.

The next morning, Anthony's suitcases, trunk and a few boxes were packed and sitting in the hallway. He stood in the doorway and looked back into the dorm room for the last time. Two beds, two empty dressers, two desks—one with a large chip in the corner of the linoleum desktop. The bare cinderblock walls painted white. A few empty clothes hangers swayed rhythmically on the bar in his closet sounding like a soft, tinny wind chime. Still there was no Don. His bed looked slept in, and some of his stuff still needed to be packed. But Anthony hadn't seen in him in several days.

Looking out the window at the far end of the room, he wondered what lay ahead for him as he closed and locked the door. He walked down the hallway and turned in his key to Jeff, the LGA. Jeff wished him well.

CHAPTER 30
New Digs

The sun was out and the air was warm. A Beach Boys song was coming from a stereo somewhere nearby. Lugging his suitcases and trunk up the one flight of stairs, Anthony looked down at the swimming pool in the middle of the Bayside apartment complex. Two hot-looking girls were lying out on lounge chairs by the pool. He carried his luggage along the walkway to apartment 18-B. The door was propped open and Anthony stumbled through the doorway. The walls were Navajo-white. The kitchen was on the left, the living area on the right, two bedrooms and a bath behind the living room. Half sitting, half lying on the worn sofa in the living room was Don.

"Man, did you see the chicks by the pool? This place is so cool. We're gonna have a blast here Bro. Way better than our old dorm up the street."

"I think you're right," Anthony agreed. "And hey! Nice job NOT helping me haul all this shit down the hill from the dorms!"

"Hey, I was on my way, when one of those girls asked me to put some more suntan lotion on her back— what can I say?" Don replied and smiled apologetically.

"And where have you been? I've been looking all over for you. Your stuff is still up in the room!" said Anthony.

"I know. I have been finishing that damn Engineering project. I should be done with it this afternoon. And Jeff said if I could get my stuff out by tomorrow morning that would be cool. I just came down here to get the room key from the manager and take a look at the place," Don replied.

Later that evening, as Anthony was emptying the last box and tossing it aside thinking it was empty, he heard something slide across the bottom of it. He picked it up again and found the old broken wristwatch. He took it out of the box and tossed it in the back of a desk drawer.

Then, he sorted through a stack of paperwork he had sitting on the desk. He pulled out a typed letter, crumpled it up in his hand and tossed it in the overflowing trashcan. As it lay on top of the heap, the crinkled corner read, "Anthony: Thank you for your transfer application to Southwestern State University..."

One's destiny does eventually reveal itself. Often it just takes time.

EPILOGUE

Don graduated from Sequoia State in 1978 and went on to get his master's degree at U.C. Berkley and became an architect in San Francisco. He got married and had two boys. They named one son, Joseph after his brother. The other one, they named Anthony after the man who had saved Don's life.

Randall and Keisha graduated from Sequoia State and soon after were married, very much against his mother's wishes. He works for as an investment broker in Southern California where Keisha helps her elderly parents.

Flynn graduated and went to work at an REI store in the boot and shoe section. He eventually became a store manager in San Diego.

Natalie's father passed away just after Christmas in 1975. Her mother still lives in Ventura. Natalie transferred to U.C. Santa Barbara and today works for the State of California in Sacramento.

Kathy Northwood graduated, got married and lives just north of Atlanta where she is in the U.S. Congress representing the 7th District of Georgia. Her office is on the third floor of a ten-story building, but the windows do not open.

Tyrone and Dylan went into business together and own a successful ice cream shop in Denver, Colorado. They hope to offer franchises soon.

No one knows what happened to Vance.

Mary Sue transferred from Sequoia State to the state university near her home in Washington. A year before she graduated, she married Jim and became Mary Sue Chandler-Martin, fulfilling her destiny.

Anthony is still looking for his.

Many Years Later
A small group of well dressed, mostly older people were sitting in the small chapel of the local funeral home. Joni Mitchell's song, "Clouds" was just concluding when an attractive middle-aged woman approached the lectern. She turned on the power and adjusted the height of the microphone. Smoothing out the paper on which she had written her speech, she gathered her composure and began.

EULOGY

"My father was born in 1956. He grew up in Southern California and graduated from Valley High School. He went away to college and attended Sequoia State University. After college, he became a high school teacher and coach. It is while he was teaching that he met our mother, who was also a teacher. He said when they met; he knew it was their destiny to be together. He said that she was his soul mate. They were married for 61 years. My brother was born first and three years later I came along.

"My dad was a great husband, father, and grandfather. As busy as he was with teaching and coaching, he always had time to play with my brother and me. We enjoyed going to his football games. He was always an assistant coach but never a head coach. He always said, 'You have to be crazy to want to be head coach.' He enjoyed working for several head coaches over the years and they seemed to think a lot of him. In fact, three of his former head coaches are present today to honor him. On behalf of my mother, brother, and myself—we appreciate you being here."

Three very old gentlemen sitting together nodded in acknowledgment.

"He told me once that he took no satisfaction in beating another team by a lopsided score. On the other hand, his greatest coaching satisfaction was coaching an underdog team and upsetting a heavily favored team. He really enjoyed that.

"Growing up, my brother and I used to enjoy hearing his stories about when he was a kid, or his college years, or his coaching stories. And Dad would enjoy telling us about his time at Sequoia State. Dumping the bucket of water on Igor; the Big Game; stealing the bear statue from the Highway Patrol were all repeated through the years. 'Yeah Dad, we remember that one,' we'd say.'"

An old man named Don, who was sitting in the first row, smiled.

"Later, when we realized his memory was fading, I would let him repeat his stories to see if any of the details changed—and they never did. However, in his final years, he couldn't remember any of the stories. In fact, we would entertain him by telling him his stories. He would laugh and ask, 'Did I really do that?'

"A few years ago, we brought Mom and Dad to live with us. Dad's memory was going fast, but he enjoyed working a little in the yard. We planted some grape vines of different varieties on the side of the house and he tended to them. It was funny; he cared for all of them, but for some reason, the Chablis vine he cared for most tenderly.

"We will miss Dad, but he will always be a part of our lives. He had a huge impact...

Made in United States
Orlando, FL
17 February 2024

43800784R00124